"It is a great honour to present you my betrothed, Miss Julie Britton,"

Prince Erik announced.

An expectant hush spread over the crowded ballroom.

Erik looked down at Julie. "What are they waiting for?" he asked softly.

She gave him a smile so sweet, it made something in him ache. "I think they're waiting for us to seal the deal," she said, almost apologetically. "With a kiss."

A *kiss.* He gathered her into his arms. Slowly she leaned toward him, her lips hovering just below his.

Erik covered her mouth with his and became lost in the reality of a kiss as sweet and warm as new honey.

He took a step back. The applause rose to a thunderous pitch, filling the massive room from wall to wall.

It was over. The crowd believed. Erik's duty to the king was done.

But his engagement to Julie was just beginning....

Dear Reader,

This month, Silhouette Romance has six irresistible, emotional and heartwarming love stories for you, starting with our FABULOUS FATHERS title, *Wanted: One Son* by Laurie Paige. Deputy sheriff Nick Dorelli had watched the woman he loved marry another and have that man's child. But now, mother and child need Nick. Next is *The Bride Price* by bestselling author Suzanne Carey. Kyra Martin has fuzzy memories of having just married her Navajo ex-fiancé in a traditional wedding ceremony. And when she discovers she's expecting his child, she knows her dream was not only real...but had mysteriously come true! We also have two not-to-be-missed new miniseries starting this month, beginning with *Miss Prim's Untamable Cowboy*, book 1 of THE BRUBAKER BRIDES by Carolyn Zane. A prim image consultant tries to tame a very masculine working-class wrangler into the true Texas millionaire tycoon he really is. Good luck, Miss Prim!

In *Only Bachelors Need Apply* by Charlotte Maclay, a man-shy woman's handsome new neighbor has some secrets that will make her the happiest woman in the world, and in *The Tycoon and the Townie* by Elizabeth Lane, a struggling waitress from the wrong side of the tracks is romanced by a handsome, wealthy bachelor. Finally, our other new miniseries, ROYAL WEDDINGS by Lisa Kaye Laurel. The lovely caretaker of a royal castle finds herself a prince's bride-to-be during a ball...with high hopes for happily ever after in *The Prince's Bride*.

I hope you enjoy all six of Silhouette Romance's terrific novels this month...and every month.

Regards,

Melissa Senate,
Senior Editor

Please address questions and book requests to:
Silhouette Reader Service
U.S.: 3010 Walden Ave., P.O. Box 1325, Buffalo, NY 14269
Canadian: P.O. Box 609, Fort Erie, Ont. L2A 5X3

THE PRINCE'S BRIDE

Lisa Kaye Laurel

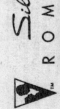

Silhouette

R O M A N C E™

Published by Silhouette Books

America's Publisher of Contemporary Romance

For my wonderful parents, who have always believed in me.

SILHOUETTE BOOKS

ISBN 0-373-19251-7

THE PRINCE'S BRIDE

Copyright © 1997 by Lisa Rizoli

This edition published by arrangement with Harlequin Books S.A.

Printed in U.S.A.

Books by Lisa Kaye Laurel

Silhouette Romance

The Groom Maker #1107
Mommy for the Moment #1173
The Prince's Bride #1251

*Royal Weddings

LISA KAYE LAUREL

has worked in a number of fields, but says that nothing she's done compares to the challenges—and rewards—of being a full-time mom. Her extra energy is channeled into creating stories. She counts writing high on her list of blessings, which is topped by the love and support of her husband, her son, her daughter, her mother and her father.

Prologue

Julie entered the castle door and found herself in the middle of a fairy tale.

She looked around, enraptured. Everything was just as she had pictured it would be when she had dreamed of dressing up and going to a royal ball at the Anders Point castle. But this was no dream. She was really here, literally rubbing elbows in the entry hall with some of the most famous and influential people in the world. It struck her that tonight, these were her peers. Though she was sixteen years old and granddaughter of the castle caretaker, she was an invited guest at the royal ball, the same as they were. Handing her wrap to an attendant, she cast a nervous glance at the mirror that hung on the wall. An attractive young woman dressed in an elegant long gown looked back at her, and Julie's first thought was, *I'd like to be friends with her.* Her second, which came with a shock, was, *I am that woman!*

Following the crowd, she took her place in the receiving line. King Ivar, who had known her from the cradle, gave her a look of approval as he took her hand. Then she was on her own. She found a place to stand at one side of the ballroom, drawing herself up straight and trying to feel as poised on the inside as the mirror had told her she looked on the outside. She had no thought of being the belle of the ball. Even to turn one head was too much to hope for. Just being there in the room with him was enough.

After all, every good fairy tale has a handsome prince, and Julie's was no exception. One glimpse of him from across the crowded ballroom kicked off a frantic fluttering in her chest. She still wasn't used to the strange and wondrous feeling she got whenever she was near Prince Erik. His very presence was magnetic. Her eyes simply couldn't look away from him; her ears strained for the sound of his voice; her skin tingled at the thought of his touch; and something inside her felt helplessly drawn toward him, as if caught by the mysterious pull of a current in the ocean. She had no idea how long she stood there, wholly absorbed in watching his fluid movements as he danced partner after partner around the floor. She rejoiced that it was his duty to dance with the most prominent of his father's guests, because it kept him within sight on the ballroom floor. He didn't notice her standing there, drinking him in with her eyes. But then, there was no reason that he should.

Near the end of a song, someone jostled into Julie, and she stepped on the hem of her gown. That brought her out of her fog. She pushed the long folds of her dress out behind her, looking over her shoulder to make sure nothing had torn. Assured that all was well, she turned back around, her gaze finding Prince Erik like the needle of a compass finds north.

He was looking at her. When their eyes met, it was like a physical touch. Julie's heart thumped so hard it hurt. She tried to take a breath but her lungs seemed frozen. Time ceased as he made his way through the crowd, never taking his eyes from her. When at last he reached her, he bowed formally.

Hours of practice in front of her bedroom mirror had paid off, and Julie executed a perfect curtsy even with jelly-filled knees.

At the sound of his voice, warmth uncurled in the pit of her stomach. "Please allow me to introduce myself," he said. "I am Erik Anders."

Julie's eyes widened. Had her transformation been so complete that he didn't know who she was? "I know," she said, offering him a tremulous smile. "I mean, you and I..." She took a deep breath and began again. "We've met before, Your Highness."

He stared at her then. "Julie? Julie Britton?"

"Yes, Your Highness."

The shock of recognition in Erik's deep, brown eyes told her that he had remembered her as the coltish teenager she had been the last time he'd seen her. His expression never changed, but his silent gaze made her feel all the more like the ugly duckling that had turned into a swan.

The silence began to feel awkward. Wasn't it his turn to say something, since she had spoken last? Feeling as if she were playing a game whose rules were written in another language, Julie said, "The ball...it's wonderful. And you dance so...beautifully." At her words she felt her cheeks grow hot. What a stupid thing to say to a prince! And *what* a time to blush! She looked away, both hoping and dreading that he would excuse himself and find his next partner, leaving her in her pink-cheeked misery to watch him from afar. But the sound of his voice drew her eyes back to his.

Up close he was so heart-stoppingly handsome that it took a moment for the words he spoke to register with her. And those words were magical. "Would you do me the honor of dancing with me?" he asked softly.

She looked at him in disbelief. Could it be true? Prince Erik wanted to dance with her! All of the fervent, silent longings of her heart had come true. Almost paralyzed with nervousness, she managed to loosen her tongue to answer. "Thank you for the kind invitation, Your Highness," she said, regaining her poise. "It would be a pleasure to dance with you."

She placed her hand on the arm he held out to her, the feel of hard muscle under his tuxedo jacket sending a warm thrill coursing through her. As he led her onto the dance floor, a sudden panic seized her—which hand was she supposed to give him to hold? She had practiced dancing with her girlfriend Drew, but they had taken turns leading, so that both ways seemed natural to Julie. Her alarm was needless, though; his movements were so smooth and sure that without her realizing quite how it happened, she was in his arms.

With all she was feeling, it was impossible for Julie to concentrate on the steps she had practiced, but she found that she didn't need to. Dancing with Erik seemed effortless; following his lead, as natural as breathing.

He held her away from him, as if she were both fragile and priceless. "Are you all right?" he asked. Julie wanted to laugh out loud. Whatever she had imagined her prince might say during a dance, it was not those words of careful concern. Was she all right? It was like asking the sun if it felt lukewarm. She let her answer beam out in a smile that seemed to melt away some of his reserve. He broadened his steps, sweeping her across the ballroom, naturally tightening his embrace and pulling her closer.

Her poise gave way as a wild restlessness swirled through her, and it seemed to Julie as though she had discovered all of the wonder of life right there in his arms. The sureness of his step as he guided her, the hardness of his muscle under her touch, even the subtle fragrance of his aftershave were constant reminders to her that this was a man who was holding her—not an almost man, like the boys at school, and not a fairy-tale prince—a real man. And she found herself responding to him like a woman, for the first time. Her body became soft and pliant, her curves nestling against his solid muscle; her insides went warm and liquid; and she couldn't look at his mouth without licking her lips. It was as if her body had been dormant and was now gradually coming to glorious life.

After what seemed a lifetime—or was it the blink of an eye?—the song came to an end. She looked up at Erik, and when their eyes met he pulled her closer. All around them couples were talking and walking, but amid the flow they stood like an island, silent and motionless, locked in an embrace. The intensity of the moment was almost overwhelming for Julie, and she knew instinctively that she could not be feeling something so powerful all by herself.

Strains of the next song filtered through, a slow song. Julie had no thought but to remain in his arms all night, but the music seemed to be a kind of a signal for Erik. He pulled back and excused himself abruptly, murmuring something about his duty as a member of the host family. Julie watched him disappear into the crowd, then made a sudden departure of her own, out of one of the French doors that lined the side of the ballroom.

Once outside, she gravitated toward the sanctuary of her secret place on the castle grounds, a rocky ledge above the ocean that was secluded from sight by trees. Alone at last, she clamped one hand over her galloping heart, which did nothing to stop it from carrying her, in her mind, at a breakneck pace over beautiful and terrifying new ground. And deep breaths of the brisk ocean air did not purge her feeling that one dance with Erik Anders had shifted the axis of her world forever and always.

She heard a noise behind her and turned to see a man leaning against a tree. With an easy movement, he started toward her.

It was Erik.

"What are you doing here?" she asked, taken by surprise. "Did you follow me?"

"No. I was here first." His voice was a deep rumble beside her in the dark.

"I didn't know anyone else knew about this place."

"I've always known."

He said no more, but just having him so near was unsettling. At last curiosity overcame her. "Why did you come out here, Erik?" she asked.

"Probably for the same reason you did."

Her heart began to pound. She knew why she was there, and she saw her feelings mirrored in his eyes. But she needed to hear him say it, to have him put it into words. "And what reason is that?" she asked softly.

He tore his gaze away from hers and turned it to the ocean. After a pause he said, "To get a breath of fresh air, of course."

Disappointed, Julie looked out over the edge of the rocks. She sensed that, here with Erik, she was poised on the brink of a chasm. She could take the no-risk path by turning away. Or she could try to make a breathtaking leap into the wonderful future that was beckoning to her from the other side.

Logic never had a chance. Julie, not wanting to live with the specter of might-have-been, took a leap of faith. "There's something I have to say to you, Erik," she said, and swallowed once before baring her soul. "I've never felt this way before. But I've had feelings for you—from afar—for a long time. And now it felt like something...happened between us, there in the ballroom."

"We shared a dance, Julie."

"There *was* more to it than that."

"Yes, there certainly was," he said, frustration roughening his voice. He turned to face her. "There was the fact that the dance was at a royal ball, in a castle. There was the fact that you are very young and are no doubt inclined to see romance lurking around every corner, anyway. There was the fact that I am an older man, five years older than you, and a prince to boot."

She couldn't help smiling. "I may be younger than you are, but there's no need to insult me. I know what I feel, and it's *not* because of any of those things."

"I'm not only older, I'm also more experienced than you are, Julie. Listen to me," he said earnestly, as if trying to convince himself. "Take away those rather unusual circumstances, and you'll realize, as I do, that it was just an ordinary dance.''

He didn't convince her; rather, his denial made her more sure that she was right. She shook her head. ''I don't think so. I believe that it was much more. And I think that you believe it, too.''

''I don't, and I'll prove it to you,'' he said, pulling her into his arms. This time it was not a charming request, but a hoarse command. ''Dance with me.''

His gruffness made her hopes soar, but he remained completely self-possessed, holding her at arm's length in an excruciatingly proper dance position. She knew what he was trying to do. There was no ballroom here, just the looming shadows of trees behind them and the endless dark expanse of the ocean in front of them. There was no sparkling light from crystal chandeliers, just the milky darkness of a night lit by a half moon. There was no sweet throatiness of an orchestra's music, just eerie wisps of melody carried their way by the restless, chilly breeze.

But none of that mattered, any more than Julie's in-experience did. Instinctively she closed the gap be-tween them, her body coming into full contact with his. She was rewarded by the sizzle of a connection, and felt his arms gather her closer. The spark took hold, becoming a fire that warmed their embrace. She felt the power of its heat as surely as she felt the thrill of being held against him.

''Do you believe there's more now?'' she asked softly.

During the long silence that followed, they aban-doned all pretense of dancing and stood poised, eyes locked, connected in body and in something more. The amber flame she saw deep in his eyes told her that she was right, that he did feel what she felt. She looked up at him, willing him to go that one step further and tell her with the kind of kiss that sealed destinies.

"You do believe, Erik," she whispered urgently. "I know you do."

With her words she saw the burning intensity in his eyes flicker and disappear. And then he kissed her—on the top of the head. He took a step backward, breaking all contact between them.

"I believe," he said evenly, "that it's time I got you back to the ballroom. I have neglected my duty long enough."

And with that her leap of faith ended with a heart-rending crash. Keeping her head high, silently fighting back tears, Julie let him escort her back to the ball. And then she walked away, through the crowded ballroom and out the front door of the castle once again, wondering why her handsome prince didn't know that fairy tales were supposed to have happy endings.

Chapter One

Erik Anders turned his back on the hospital bed to look out the window, not that he noticed the view of Boston spread out before him. He was taking a moment to remind himself that the man lying in the bed behind him was King Ivar, ruler of Isle Anders, a man to whom deference was due even when he wasn't lying in recovery from heart surgery.

He had to remind himself because, at that moment, His Majesty the king was acting like your basic, garden variety, stubbornly infuriating father. *His* father.

"I await your answer," came the king's commanding voice from behind him.

Prince Erik turned back and took his seat at his father's bedside. On the other side of the bed sat his younger brother, Whit, who looked both amused and relieved that Erik had drawn their father's fire this time.

"Your Majesty, perhaps this is not the best time to discuss this." Erik's voice kept its customary calm. The king's doctor had made it clear to him and his brother that although their father was making progress in his recovery, they had to make every effort to keep him from feeling stress of any kind.

The king, who did not take to coddling, gave Erik a smoldering look. "You, my elder son, are the crown prince of Isle Anders. Destiny has chosen you to succeed me to the throne," he said. "I place great trust in you, and never have you let me down. Never have you shirked a duty. Until now."

Erik counted to ten in his native language and then in English before answering. "With all due respect, sire, I am not shirking this duty, either. I am well aware that the laws of tradition dictate that the crown prince of Isle Anders must take a bride before being crowned king, and I stand ready to uphold that requirement."

"You are thirty years old. Just when do you plan to fulfill your duty?" the king demanded.

"Before my coronation, which I hope will not take place for a good many years."

"I am getting older," the king warned. "I just had major surgery."

"From which your doctor expects you will make a fine recovery," Erik stated calmly. "All you need to do is rest."

"I can't rest easy until I know the succession is secure."

"It will be." Erik reminded himself that his father was only thinking about the country they both loved. Isle Anders wasn't big, but it was beautiful, a jewel of an island in the deep blue waters of the North Atlantic, not far from Iceland. During the short summer it glowed with the dark green fire of an emerald; in winter it sparkled with the icy brilliance of a diamond. It was icier than Greenland, greener than Iceland, and its people were as gutsy and strong as the Vikings who had first populated it. The Anders family, which had acquired its wealth independent of its position, had ruled the island with pride for countless years with the approval of the citizens they served. The way Erik looked at it, he had been born into the privilege of doing a job he loved, and he would do nothing to jeopardize that. Like his father, Erik Anders took his duty to Isle Anders very seriously.

"Without a marriage, there can be no heir to the throne," the king pointed out.

"I assure you, sire—" Erik began.

"I am not assured!" Fire flashed from behind the king's blue eyes. "I know that there is no shortage of admiring women around you, but I am also well aware that you don't give any of them the slightest chance to win your affection. And as for him—" The king threw a glance of reproof at Whit, who had such a reputation as a ladies' man that the press had dubbed him the Prince of Hearts. "Where does this leave me? With one son who refuses to fall in love and another who falls in love every other week!" he said, his voice echoing off the walls of the room.

Then, as quickly as it had arisen, the fire in the king's eyes died. He sank back heavily against his pillows, his face ashen, just as his doctor entered the room.

"You two, out of here!" the doctor ordered sharply. Both princes jumped to the command. All three men knew that in the matter of the king's health, the doctor's status as a medical man outranked the princes' royalty.

Out in the hallway Erik and his brother exchanged a worried look.

"Do you think he's all right?" Whit finally asked.

Erik shrugged and propped a shoulder against the wall.

Whit dragged his fingers through his hair. "I hate to see him like this."

Erik knew what he meant. The golden strands of the king's thick hair and beard were well-laced with silver, and his recent illness and surgery had left him looking careworn and haggard. And the way he talked.... For the first time, Erik feared his indomitable father might be giving up hope. The thought gave him a bone-deep chill.

He shook it off, refusing to think about the possibility of King Ivar's not making it. Instead of dwelling on something he had no power over, he turned his thoughts to something he did: his father's preoccupation with the idea of securing the succession. Erik had long known that it was his duty to his country to marry before his coronation. But maybe it was his duty to his father to do it sooner.

He had someone in mind, of course; someone he had known for a long time. She was exactly the kind of woman he had always expected to take as a wife: a woman who suited him perfectly, who surely shared his feeling that she was destined to be his bride.

Erik had waited for a number of reasons, but now he knew that he had put off the inevitable long enough. The time was finally right. Tonight's ball would be the perfect forum for him to introduce his future bride to the world. The perfect setting for their rendezvous with destiny.

Julie Britton set down the receiver but hung on to the phone, as if that might stop the strange soaring feeling that the unexpected news had given her.

Of course she had known Prince Erik would be back in the States, now that his father was ill. But she never expected that he would make an appearance at the ball here in Anders Point tonight.

Not that it mattered to her, Julie told herself firmly. She was in charge of planning the charity ball for King Ivar. She had overseen everything, right down to the last detail. It couldn't possibly matter to her which of the king's sons was to perform the duties of host.

In the past it had always been Prince Whit who oversaw these glamorous high-publicity events, while Erik tended to shy away from the spotlight. She wondered now what could possibly be forcing the mysterious Prince Erik away from desk duty and out into the public.

Under her hand the phone rang again. Julie jumped, then answered.

"Hello?"

"Julie! What are you still doing there at the castle?" It was her friend, Annah. "Not much," Julie said dryly. "Just planning a royal ball."

"Well, it's ten hours to midnight, Cinderella. Are you going to come down here and pick out a gown, or were you planning on wearing your rags to the ball?"

"Ten hours to—omigosh! It's two o'clock already? I'll be right there, Annah. Bye!"

After a quick check with the head chef on the food preparation for the evening, Julie rushed from the castle, carefully securing the door behind her. Not that she was worried about a break-in. The tiny coastal town of Anders Point, Maine, was hardly a hotbed of criminal activity. But she took great pride in her job as castle caretaker, treating the stately mansion as if it were her home. Of course it wasn't her castle; it belonged to King Ivar.

But it felt like it was hers, because Julie was the only one who had lived there for the past year, except for occasional visits by the king. He had asked her to take over as caretaker after the death of her grandfather, who had long held the position. The decision was a no-brainer for Julie, who had lived in New York City since the age of three, but had spent most summers at Anders Point with her grandfather. The king's offer had given her the ideal setup. Her duties had allowed her to continue her career as a reading specialist—she had gotten a part-time position in the town school, which had let out the week before for summer vacation—and she had a place to live.

Not just any place. She paused to look up at the magnificent facade, pushing away wisps of hair that the breeze from the ocean had freed from her braid. The castle, perched on a rocky bluff at the tip of Anders Point, was magical. It was built more for function than form, but it had a raw, elemental beauty set off by the backdrop of the restless ocean. Inside, its stone walls and dark corridors oozed history and romance.

No wonder she had once fallen in love there.

But that incredible night seemed like a dream now. She hadn't seen Erik since their moonlit dance, nine years ago. But even now, Julie still cringed at the memory. She had crashed, all right, but in time she'd picked herself up and gone on with her life.

Preoccupied with her thoughts, she walked slowly around the castle, smiling wistfully at her long-ago hopes for what might have been with Erik. It hadn't worked out, but she didn't regret her decision to take a chance. There had been no happy ending for her, but she still believed in love.

The castle brought out her romantic nature. Especially since it was here that King Ivar himself had fallen in love, when he was still a prince. It was his family's get-away home, and he had been staying in it while on official business in America, when a girl from Anders Point had captured his heart. She had been similarly smitten, and their storybook romance and royal wedding had thrilled the world, and Julie, too. She herself hadn't been born when it happened, of course, but she had begged her mother time and again to tell the story of how the girl her mother had once jumped rope with had grown up to become a princess; and then a queen when Ivar took the throne.

In the queen's memory, the king held a huge ball every few years at the Anders Point castle where they had met, to raise money for her favorite charity. The sweetness of that gesture always touched Julie, who saw it as undeniable proof that even a man as powerful and demanding as King Ivar could be as romantic as she was on the inside—unlike his son. Naturally, the king himself had always hosted the ball. And although he wouldn't be there this time, he had insisted that the ball go on as scheduled.

Tonight. It was hard to believe. It seemed like only a million details ago that the king had asked her to be in charge of coordinating the preparations for the ball. Julie, who had never so much as planned a wedding, had been flattered by the king's trust in her, and was determined to prove that it had not been misplaced.

Especially now, with him in the hospital. She had been fond of the king ever since she was a little girl. During the past year her regard had grown. Julie figured she would do just about anything to ease the king's mind and speed his recovery.

With that thought, she hurried to her car and drove down the hill on the castle road. Julie made herself take deep breaths of the breeze coming in off the ocean. To her knowledge, no one had ever died of excitement, but she didn't want to be the first, not today of all days. Not when she finally had a chance to get a glimpse of Prince Erik again.

"Julie! Julie!" Six-year-old Lexi Davis sprinted out from the back room of the two-story house Annah lived and worked in. The little girl's hands clamped an aluminum foil tiara, which had been knocked askew by her run, onto the top of her head.

"Princess Lexi! How was your morning?" Julie asked as she caught her up in a hug. Lexi's mother, Julie's childhood friend Drew, was sheriff of Anders Point. To the dismay of her practical mother, Lexi's princess phase had far outlived that of most other little girls. Lexi didn't just play princess; she lived it. Julie, who considered such imagination a priceless gift, happily indulged her.

"It was—," Lexi paused, frowning, no doubt thinking of a word with just the right amount of royal condescension. "Quite satisfactory," she finished with a smile.

"I'm pleased to hear it, Your Highness."

"Because this is the *best* place to play dress up," Lexi added breathlessly. "I love when Annah watches me."

"Where's your mommy?"

"Out on a call."

That could mean anything, Julie knew. As the town's

only elected official, Drew was a combination sheriff, justice of the peace, animal control officer and settler of trivial disputes between neighbors.

Lexi was still chattering as they walked past Annah's coffee counter and into her secondhand shop in back. Like the one when the princess saved the kingdom from the dragon?''

''Can you make up another fairy tale with me, Julie?

''I don't have time, honey. Tonight's the ball.''

Lexi sighed. ''You get to live in the castle, *and* you get to go to the ball. You're the luckiest person in the world.''

Julie smiled at her. ''I think I am,'' she agreed.

They walked into a tiny room in back, which Annah used as her office. Annah, who was just hanging up the phone, smiled at Julie.

''You look like you just swallowed fireworks,'' she said.

Julie shrugged happily, eyes sparkling. ''I *am* going to a royal ball tonight.''

''Yes, I know,'' Annah teased. ''Maybe you'll be swept off your feet by a movie star or a diplomat or a multibillionaire——''

''Or a prince,'' Lexi suggested.

''In my dreams,'' Julie said with a laugh. At least, in her dreams of long ago.

''Are you wearing anything in those dreams?'' Annah asked dryly. ''I don't know how you could leave your dress for the last minute like this, but better late than never.''

''I have great faith in you. I knew you would find me something,'' Julie said.

''Two somethings,'' Julie said. With a smile, Annah turned to a closet in the corner of the office and pulled out a short, strapless dress of brilliant blue. "Ta-da. What do you think?"

Julie looked at it. "Ah," she said, noncommittally. "And the other something?"

Annah sighed, and rummaged another dress out of the closet. "This," she said, holding up a black gown with sheer sleeves and a floor-length hem.

Julie looked at them both. "What do you think?"

"No contest. The blue," Annah said. "It's made for you, Julie. You're the only woman I know who could do it justice."

Julie looked at the dress doubtfully. "It *is* gorgeous, Annah. But I've heard you can never go wrong with basic black."

"Black is all wrong for your coloring. No one has bluer eyes than you do, Julie, and this dress will make them shine more than the most exquisite jewels in that ballroom."

Uh-oh. Annah was starting to wax poetic about the darn dress, which, Julie noticed, barely covered the hanger. "It doesn't look my size," she pointed out diplomatically.

Annah thrust the dress into her hands. "Trust me."

Julie sighed. Annah knew her way around clothes. She had an instinct for knowing what looked good on all of her customers, which was why they kept coming back. And she herself always looked terrific. Annah had class.

She was smiling brightly at Julie. "Try it on," she urged.

Minutes later, Julie emerged from the dressing room and looked at Annah, waiting for her reaction.

"Oh, Julie," Annah said, her dark eyes wide. "Even I didn't expect it was going to look this good."

Lexi stared at Julie, openmouthed, before bestowing on her the highest compliment in her six-year-old world. "You look like a *real* princess," she said.

"Now let's try something out on your hair," Annah said, starting in with a brush.

While she was working, the bell on the front door jangled. Lexi flew out to see who had come into the store. "Mommy!" Julie heard her say. "Come see Princess Julie!"

"Drew, stay out there until I'm finished," Annah called. "I want you to get the full effect."

"She won't let me look, either," complained Julie. She was glad Drew had arrived in time to give her opinion. They had been friends forever, playing together all those summers she had visited her grandfather. They'd had the run of the castle grounds, a kid's paradise, and had been joined by Prince Whit whenever he and the king stayed at the castle. Whit was Julie's age, Drew just a year younger, and in those days the three had been as inseparable as the peanut butter and marshmallow goop sandwiches that had been their favorite lunch. But Julie hadn't seen Whit since they were both sixteen, while she'd seen Drew every summer but one.

"How is everything going for the ball, Julie?" Drew asked her.

"So far, so good, keep your fingers crossed."

More quietly, Drew said, "When does Whit arrive?"

"Not Whit. Erik." As she said his name, Julie felt her stomach give a funny lurch to zero gravity.

"Prince Erik?" Drew sounded surprised. "I thought Whit was going to take the king's place as host."

"He was supposed to, but I just got a call from one of King Ivar's men. It'll be Erik." It still seemed strange to think that Erik would be at the ball tonight. After all those years, she would see him again. She couldn't help wondering what would happen. Maybe they would dance, and maybe the magic she remembered would be recaptured, and this time, maybe... Amazed at the rapidity of her chain of thought, Julie was forced to smile at her own expense. More likely he'd pat her on the head and send her away again.

"I'm surprised that Whit would pass up the chance to host a ball," Drew said. "Talk about being in his element. Glitz, glamour, publicity, beautiful women..."

"I wonder why Prince Erik hasn't married yet," Annah mused. "Do you think he's looking for a bride, Julie?"

The king had made no secret to Julie of his great desire to have his older son marry, but Julie had no idea what Erik's opinion on the matter was. "If he is, he should hire you as a consultant, Annah," she told her friend warmly. Annah had an uncanny talent for spotting true love when she saw it. "Would you like me to suggest it to him tonight?"

Annah laughed. "Why don't you go for him yourself, and avoid the middleman?"

"If the past is any indication, she doesn't need any encouragement, Annah," Drew said from the other room.

Julie ignored the hot blush that Drew's teasing comment had called up and spoke to Annah. "Childhood friends remember the most inconvenient things." Like an embarrassing crush on a friend's older brother.

Annah put the brush down. "This sounds interesting," she said. "Do tell."

Julie gave a sheepish grin. "I kind of fell for Erik," she explained.

"When?" asked Annah.

"Ages ago," Julie said, secure in the knowledge that now she was neither so young nor so naive. At sixteen, she had thought she'd found the love of her life, but he had obviously not felt the same inexorable pull of destiny that she had. At twenty-five she hardly spent her days pining over him.

Still, to be honest, she had to admit that she seemed unable to erase him from her mind completely. She had always wondered what would happen if she got a grown-up chance to see whether her young intuition had been on target. The king's change of plans had given her an excellent opportunity to satisfy her curiosity. Naturally she had no real expectations; but Julie was an incurable optimist, and optimism sometimes has very little to do with what is realistic. Somewhere inside her lived the battered, but still breathing, hope that someday, somehow, she might have another chance to try to win Erik's heart. And she knew that seeing him tonight at the ball would either resuscitate that hope or give it the blow that would lay it to rest for good.

Uncannily Drew read her thoughts. "You aren't really interested in him, are you, Julie?" She sounded concerned.

Julie didn't answer.

"Everyone has things that they keep from even their best friends," observed Annah as she put the finishing touches on Julie's hair.

It was true, Julie knew. Annah herself avoided any reminders of the painful circumstances surrounding her divorce. And Drew never talked about Lexi's father; had in fact kept his identity a secret, even from them.

Close as the three were, they respected each other's privacy.

"You can come in now, Drew," Annah said at last.

Drew stopped in the doorway and stood there, staring, while Julie turned around in the middle of the room. Drew was the most down-to-earth person she knew. If Julie looked like a hooker on a holiday, Drew would have no qualms about telling her so.

"Well, Drew?" Julie said.

"You're absolutely stunning, kid. Didn't know you had it in you."

"That makes two of us," Julie said, staring at her reflection in the floor-length mirror Annah steered her over to. She hardly recognized herself, with her hair up like this. Annah had been right about what the color of the dress would do for her eyes, too. As for the dress itself, it was a bit of shapely, shimmering magic, hugging curves that Julie hadn't realized she had. She swallowed. "But isn't it a little on the——"

"Sexy side?" Drew supplied.

"Omigosh. Too sexy?"

"Not too sexy," Annah assured her quickly. "Classy sexy. Understated sexy."

Drew rolled her eyes. "Understated? When she walks through that ballroom, testosterone levels will hit the danger zone."

Julie knew that Drew, who never exaggerated, must be doing it now—even though it was a heady thought.

"Every woman needs a night like that in her life," Annah said.

"I'm not really a guest at the ball," Julie reminded them and herself. "I'm the hired help. Maybe I'd better try on the black one."

She did, and wondered who ever had come up with

the idea that black was sexy and sophisticated. On her, basic black was basic boring. Worse. She looked like a cadaver.

Lexi was the first to speak. "Before you looked like a princess," she said, looking up at Julie. "Now you look like a lady-in-waiting."

"What do you two think?" Julie asked her friends.

"The blue." Annah gave her vote firmly.

"The blue," Drew agreed.

Julie looked in the mirror and decided that she was tired of being a lady-in-waiting. "All right, all right," she said laughingly. "I'll be a princess."

Julie walked into the castle kitchen and helped herself to a sample from a tray of hors d'oeuvres on the counter.

"Mmm," she said, smiling up into the frown of the head chef. "Is the rest of the food this good, Gustave?"

"How would I know?" he asked, raising one eyebrow. "I have spent the afternoon doing your job, *mademoiselle*."

"Oh, then you took care of things while I was gone?"

"Of course. And right now half of the tradesmen in America are in the ballroom awaiting your instructions."

"I knew I could count on you," Julie said, giving him an impetuous kiss on the cheek.

The phone rang. "And that's another thing," he pointed out. "*Mademoiselle*, surely even in this godforsaken corner of America you have heard of answering machines."

"I didn't think of turning it on, since you were

here," Julie said, adding impishly, "Did the phone ring while I was gone?"

"Incessantly," he said with a sniff. "I managed to ignore it, until the last time."

"Who was it?"

"His Highness, the crown prince."

Julie spun around. *Erik* called? "What did he say?"

Gustave was busy tasting a sauce that an underling held out to him on a spoon. He gave a few curt instructions, while Julie thought she would burst out of her skin, waiting.

"He said he needed to speak with you privately on an urgent matter and would call back." He nodded toward the ringing phone. "That would be he, I suppose."

Julie ran into the library and grabbed the phone. It was indeed Erik.

"Hello, Julie," he said, his deep voice setting something inside her vibrating.

Her answer was barely a whisper. "Prince Erik."

He seemed to hesitate before speaking again, and when he did, there was a new warmth in his voice. "It's…been a while."

"Yes. It has." Her stomach gave another one of those weightless lurches, as if she had swallowed a helium balloon. Ignoring it, she warned herself against reading any sentimentality into his end of the conversation. He was no doubt calling on business, now that he was hosting the ball. In a voice that she optimistically told herself sounded perfectly calm, she added, "If you're calling about tonight, the arrangements are nearly all in place."

"I imagine so. This is probably not the best time to spring a surprise on you."

"A surprise?"

"Yes," he said. "And my plans depend on you, Julie."

Something in his voice told her that he was talking about a matter of far more consequence than rearranging the seating at the ball, but she refused to allow herself to indulge in any wild speculations. "Your father places great trust in me," she assured him professionally.

"He has made no secret of that fact."

His response warmed her. "I understand you saw the king this morning," she said. "How is he?"

"Not good," he said soberly.

Julie couldn't disguise the worry in her voice. "Your Highness, what's wrong with him?"

"Nothing that I can't rectify," he said. "Medically, the king's progress has been fair, but it is being impeded by his preoccupation with the succession. Given how closely you work with him, I assume he has shared with you his great desire that I choose a bride."

"He has mentioned his—ah, concern," Julie admitted.

Erik seemed amused. "His Majesty will have no reason to question my devotion to duty, after tonight. Everything has been arranged, except for the announcement itself."

Julie frowned, puzzled. "I—I beg your pardon?"

"My father's worries will end at midnight," Erik explained. "When I announce my engagement."

Chapter Two

Alone in her tower room, the highest point in the castle, Julie looked at her hair with satisfaction. The style was cool and sophisticated, which was exactly the image she wanted to project tonight at the ball. Especially to herself.

She knew one thing as perfectly as she knew her own name: any silly hopes she had for renewing that old spark she'd felt with Prince Erik were now dead and buried.

Granted, the news of his engagement had taken her by surprise at first, but the real surprise was that it had taken him this long to surrender his status as one of the world's most eligible bachelors. He was not only crown prince of Isle Anders, he was handsome, he was intelligent, and his integrity was unparalleled. He would be a good husband to the woman he had chosen. Julie wished them well.

As for that powerful feeling she had felt with him, whatever it was it obviously meant nothing if he hadn't felt it, too. He might not even recognize her after all these years, and there was no reason to believe that he would remember a long-ago evening that he, at the time, had taken pains to prove hadn't meant anything to him. Julie sure hoped he didn't remember—her own memory of it was embarrassing enough. But even if he did, she had no fear that he would make any reference to it. His sense of honor was as strong as his sense of duty.

Erik belonged to someone else, but he wasn't going to be the only man at the ball, she reminded herself as she put on the blue dress Annah had pressed for her. She wrinkled her nose at her reflection in the mirror and gave a little rueful grin at the fanciful imaginings that had dwelt deep within her for so long.

This was the perfect dress to wear to dance on the grave of her silly dreams.

Erik stood in the ballroom doorway, looking into the cavernous stone-walled room that would in less than an hour be the setting for a royal ball, a ball people were paying fabulous amounts of money to the king's favorite charity in order to attend.

He had expected austere dignity, but what he found was a close approximation of bedlam. People carrying flowers were running back and forth, dodging others toting tables and chairs. The decorative fountain had run amok, and a group of people armed with towels were mopping up the resultant river. The head of the wait staff was giving the resultant river. The head of the instructions, punctuated with wide sweeps of both hands. Security was restless, trying to school their expressions into placidity as they watched the hubbub in the room. From the kitchen came the unmistakable bellow of his father's head chef, while the orchestra, ensconced on a makeshift stage in the front of the room, added to the chaos as it played snatches of songs for a sound check.

In the center of the swirl of activity stood Julie Britton. He hadn't seen her in years, but he would have recognized her anywhere. It was obvious that she was in charge—people kept running up to her to tell or ask her something. But she was regal and poised, by far the calmest person in the room. One encouraging word from her, and even the most frantic person left her looking confident. Maybe it was her hundred-watt smile or her obvious delight in the proceedings. Whatever it was, it was working miracles. As he watched, bedlam gradually subsided as the room transformed, surrounding Julie in beauty.

Certainly, Erik thought, she was even more beautiful than he remembered. Not that the adjective did her justice, or had much to do with the fact that she was already in formal dress. Much more than outward appearance, Julie's allure radiated from within. She was so vibrantly alive, and even from across the ballroom, the force of her appeal hit him harder than he was prepared for. It had been the same way one long-ago night; there was something about her that beckoned to him. Now, as then, he was so drawn that he found himself walking across the ballroom toward her.

Amid the frantic last-minute preparations, Julie sensed a movement that was out of place. A man was coming her way, and she didn't need the discreet nod given him by the chief of security to know that the man was Prince Erik. The confusion around her continued, but as she focused on him, her awareness of all else ceased.

Reality exceeded memory. He topped six feet by an inch or two, and it looked as if all of his weight came from lean, trim muscle. He carried himself with regal assurance; moreover, he exuded an aura of intelligent confidence that suited his tough, rangy build. Crown prince or no, he obviously spent a good deal of time outdoors, because his dark blond hair was sun streaked against his tanned skin. His dark brown eyes still had no bottom that she could discern.

He stopped in front of her, as he had nine years before. Her eyes met his unfathomable gaze, completing a circuit like an electrical connection. Now, as then, an involuntary heightening of awareness nearly bowled her over, and the two moments linked across the span of years between them. Feeling it so strongly again, she knew why she had taken a risk back then—and knew with utter certainty that she had been right to do so.

For Erik, standing so close to Julie brought back vivid memories of her naive sensuality and refreshing honesty, and of the night they had almost been too much to resist. One dance with her had had him shirking his responsibilities, rushing outside to try to regain his equilibrium. But looking for peace of mind in a spot of seclusion, he had found Julie instead. He had purposely misled her in refusing to admit that there was something between them. There had been, and that was precisely why he had backed off. Surrendering control to an unknown emotion, especially one that strong, was untenable for Erik.

Seeing her again, he was glad he'd found the strength to resist her. A woman who could make him feel like that was the wrong kind of woman for him. The years had proven him right.

With that conviction, he dismissed the past and gave her a polite, but impersonal, nod. "Hello, Julie," he said.

His perfunctory greeting called her back to the present, back from the night she had danced with him under an endless sky and had wished on every star in the galaxy that he would feel what she had.

But the stars had had better things to do. Now he was marrying someone else, and she was older and infinitely wiser. Still, she realized how much easier it had been to handle the news of his engagement over the phone. Up close it was harder to think of wishing him well in marrying another woman. Luckily she had made her congratulations on the phone, so she got right down to business.

"Good evening, Your Highness," she said formally. "What can I do for you?" It was helpful to remember that she was the employee. It was natural that he assign duties to her as he pleased, as he had occasionally done by mail and fax since the king's illness.

"After speaking with you, I made arrangements to have cameras set up in here to simulcast the ball, including the announcement, in my father's hospital room."

"You don't think the news will be too much of a shock for him?" Julie asked, concerned.

"My finally getting engaged will doubtless be a shock," Erik said dryly. "However, since it will be of a pleasant variety, his doctor has given full approval." He paused. "The camera crew will arrive any minute, and I've given them incentive to set up quickly. I hope they won't cause you any problems."

She gave him a confident smile. "None I can't handle."

"Good," he said briskly. "Has Roberta arrived?"

"Not to my knowledge."

"Then she must not be here. I told her to seek you out if she arrived before I did."

"Now that you are here," Julie said with a smile, "I am sure that you will be the first to know of her arrival."

"I doubt that," he said, matter-of-factly. "I will be quite busy with a number of things I have to do before the ball. Please keep me posted on her arrival."

"Of course." Apparently he was no romantic, who would spend the wait pacing the floor in anticipation of the arrival of his lady love.

"I'd also like a room to be prepared for her. It will be expected that she, as my fiancée, will be a guest here in the castle."

Julie thought that was a funny way of putting it. Didn't he *want* to be with her?

"She can have the bedroom at the top of the stairs," Erik went on. "I'll take the tower room that adjoins it."

Julie didn't say anything.

"Is something wrong?"

"No, Your Highness," Julie said. "I have been living in the tower room, but I'll move my things out."

He shook his head. "I don't want to put you out. The two adjoining bedrooms in the north hall will serve my purpose just as well."

"I can move. It's—"

"I insist," Erik said simply.

Julie gave in. He had an air of quiet command that he wore well, she thought. He would make a good leader.

"As you wish," she said. "Is there anything else?

Would you like to inspect the kitchen, take a quick tour of the grounds, see the list of—''

''That won't be necessary,'' he said, cutting her off. ''It's obvious that you are doing a fine job pulling things together. If I can trust you with the secret of my engagement, I can certainly trust you with the details of the evening.'' He glanced at his watch. ''I have a few details of my own to take care of now. Until later, Julie,'' he said, and departed.

Erik entered the library and closed the door behind him. It would be quiet enough in here to finish up the paperwork that he would have to get to Whit, now that his brother would be taking over for him on Isle Anders. The king had insisted that Erik stay at Anders Point for a while and take on Whit's public relations duties. His father knew Erik preferred doing the king's domestic duties, the nuts-and-bolts work of running the country, far better than the international schmoozing Whit excelled at. Erik suspected that the king, by changing his duties, was trying to pressure him to choose a bride. He hated this whole arrangement, but had reason to hope that it would only be temporary, and it paled in comparison to his fear for the king's health.

Concern about his father's recovery had been gnawing at Erik, but he was not a worrier, he was a doer. The scene at the hospital that morning had sealed his decision. It was time to get on with the matter of securing the succession. The actual marriage didn't have to take place until right before his coronation, but if Erik were engaged in the meantime, it might allay his father's concerns so that he could recover. To accomplish that, Erik would do anything in his power.

He had had an understanding with Roberta for quite some time. After all, he had known all along that eventually he would have to choose a bride. For a number of reasons, he felt she would be suitable. She was not from Isle Anders, but that was not an issue; his father had himself married a girl from Maine. Erik had known Roberta for a long time. His father thought highly of her, as did everyone who knew her. She carried herself well in public and would be able to perform all the duties that went along with being queen someday.

Her manners were refined, impeccable. She wouldn't cause him public embarrassment of any kind. Heiress to a multimillion-dollar fortune, she nevertheless stayed out of the headlines. Sophisticated and polished, she had the background and social graces to be the kind of hostess he would need for state dinners and other events. Cautious and restrained, she took life as it came, instead of rushing headlong out to meet it. With her he would find steady reliability, not breathless excitement.

Best of all, she was no more in love with him than he was with her, which made possible the only kind of marriage that he would consider—a marriage for duty. She had been in love, unrequited love, with a scoundrel who had strung her along mercilessly for years. But she had finally given up her vain hopes of marrying him. This morning she had accepted Erik's proposal and his terms for their marriage. And once she had agreed, he had no doubt that she would do her duty, as he was doing his. She was a woman of her word.

As far as expediting the matter went, circumstances were in his favor. The ball would be the perfect place to take care of this business, although the announcement was a necessary evil as far as Erik was concerned.

He was by nature a private man. But the fact that he would publicly plight his troth would assure the king he meant business; and that, Erik hoped, would speed his father's recovery.

After making a final check on the camera crew, Erik went up to his room to dress. Before he went downstairs, he placed a call.

"The king is unavailable," the head nurse in his private wing informed Erik. "He's resting up."

"Is everything in place there?"

"All hooked up, they tell me," she said.

"What did you tell the king?"

"Just what you told me to tell him, Your Highness. That you hoped he would enjoy watching the ball, even though he couldn't attend, and that you were going to make an announcement at midnight that you thought he would be interested in."

"Good. Now there's just one more thing I'd like you to do."

"Don't worry. I'll make sure he's watching," she promised.

Naturally Erik looked spectacular in a tux.

Julie greeted him when he came down the stairs. "I just want to make you aware, Your Highness, that the rumors are flying," she said.

"Rumors?"

"That you will be announcing your engagement tonight."

He swore under his breath, then apologized for it. "Where did you hear that?"

Julie pointed to the media crews gathered outside on the front lawn. The king allowed them limited access to the ball, in order to raise awareness for his charity.

And besides, most of those in attendance loved the excitement and glamour of flash bulbs exploding in their faces as they got out of their limos.

Erik's expression was grim. "How did they find out?"

"I don't know," Julie said, a little defensively.

"I didn't mean that I thought you told them," he said, impatiently. "I told you I trusted you."

"At any rate, the rumors have reached your father," she told him. "He called to ask me if I knew who his future daughter-in-law was."

"And?"

"I told him that if you hadn't told him yourself, it must not be any of his business," Julie said simply.

She looked at Erik's expression and couldn't help smiling. "You don't have to look so relieved. I thought you trusted me."

"Looks like I had good reason to," he said, giving her one of his rare smiles. "And the best part of it is, you didn't even lie to him."

Outside, the first limousine drove up to the front entryway. "Did you decide where you will be receiving guests?" she asked him.

"No, but I think he could tell I was dodging. The king knows I'd make a lousy liar."

"Where you suggested, inside the ballroom."

"I'll make security aware of the expected traffic flow."

"Fine," he said. "By the way, I'm impressed with the way everything has fallen into place so smoothly, Julie."

"Just doing my job, Your Highness."

* * *

"If your jaw were clenched any tighter, Your Highness, the muscles in your cheeks would explode."

Erik didn't have to turn around to know who spoke. Gustave had been his father's chef for years, and he had all the familiarity of a long-time employee who was a de facto member of the family. Gustave always managed to appear at these occasions as a guest, even though he was in charge of the food.

"Just doing my job as host. Making sure everyone is having a good time," Erik said, eyes on the crowded ballroom before him.

"Especially the lovely *mademoiselle* in blue, I see." Although born on Isle Anders, Gustave was half French, a circumstance that flavored both his cooking and his speech.

He was observant, too. Erik had been watching Julie all night. And he wasn't the only one. It came as no surprise to him that the eyes of some of the top connoisseurs in the world of women had glazed over when she walked into the ballroom.

"She has done a fine job," Erik said, choosing safe ground. "As for her appearance, she does much credit to the king by her manner of poise and restraint."

"Ah, yes, I have often myself been struck by her level of *poise* and *restraint*," Gustave said with a chuckle. Erik wondered what the chef found so amusing, but became distracted when he saw a duke with a reputation for shameless philandering trying to wheedle Julie onto the dance floor. A duke who, in the receiving line, had asked him who the luscious babe in blue was. It had taken all of Erik's restraint to give him a civilized, stony stare, when what he wanted to do was take him outside and wipe the leer from his face.

It was requiring even more restraint to watch the man flirt with her now. It wasn't the first time Erik had felt protective toward Julie. He could have kissed her that night nine years ago, like she'd wanted him to—hell, like *he'd* wanted to. But it wouldn't have been fair to leave her with a memory like that, young and vulnerable as she was. He had rejected her, but at least he had tried to be gentle as she was. And seeing her again, all grown up, and obviously over him, he realized that he must have handled the matter well. As much as Erik's instincts still made him want to protect Julie, reason told him he had no right to. Even if he weren't a soon-to-be engaged man.

A waiter, wending his way through the crowd, offered them champagne from his tray. Gustave took a glass and, watching the duke, asked Erik idly, "Isn't this where the prince rescues the fair damsel from the dragon?"

Erik, who had no taste for champagne, waved the waiter away. "Where have you been, my friend? Fair damsels can take care of themselves these days," he said, as much for his own benefit as for Gustave's. As if on cue, Julie went her way alone, leaving behind a crestfallen duke.

"A pity," Gustave observed. "It gave you young princes something to do."

Erik looked at Julie for the hundredth time since he'd arrived that afternoon. She carried herself with a refined grace that made her look right at home in the elegance that surrounded her. Her brown hair, swept off her bare shoulders into a smooth, sophisticated style, shone with gold and copper highlights. She wore a tasteful amount of makeup that played up her features but didn't hide the scattered freckles he remembered, and those only enhanced the glow of her skin. Curvy in her evening dress, she seemed sexy without meaning to be; but those long legs of hers would show to advantage no matter what she wore——or didn't wear.

Gustave's low voice intruded on his thoughts, which were taking a dangerous turn. "It looks like she is going to the serving tables. Would you like to join her, Your Highness? The food is excellent. I can vouch for it."

At that, Erik smiled. "I'm sure you can. Maybe later, Gustave."

"Ah, and maybe later the young lady will be dancing. She turned down the duke, but she will accept my offer. I am a grandfather, and dancing with me will be no threat to a lovely young *mademoiselle*," Gustave said, gliding away. "Of course, it will be no thrill, either. Unlike a dance with the prince."

Erik watched him disappear into the crowd. As host, it was his duty to dance with as many of the women in attendance as possible. But he wouldn't dance with Julie. He had danced with her nine years ago and had felt things that he didn't think were decent for a grown man of twenty-one to feel toward a girl of sixteen. Even worse, he had felt something much deeper than lust. Now she was of age, and he was about to be safely engaged—but he still had no intention of challenging what he had battled to overcome at twenty-one.

Julie was seating herself at one of the tiny tables set in one corner of the room, among an attractive grouping of large plants and the formerly recalcitrant fountain, which now bubbled obediently. Laughing at something a man at the next table said to her, she took a delicate bite of food, then a sip of champagne. Suddenly she glanced up, right at Erik. Caught staring, he looked guiltily away, then cursed himself both for staring at her in the first place and for having such a damn fool reaction to being caught.

Impatiently he looked toward the entrance. Surely Roberta should have been here by now. The camera crew was busy filming the ball. He had told them to expect that his surprise announcement would take place at midnight.

Not that it was going to be much of a surprise anymore, and that was all right. People were probably speculating as to his choice, and Roberta's name should be at the top of most people's list. They had dated casually for years, on and off. It had worked well because neither had expected anything from the other. She because she was in love with another man, he because he had no desire to love or be loved by any woman.

Now he was expecting a lot of her. And he was confident that she would give it. He trusted her. She would show.

Julie, alerted by the persistent ringing of the castle's private line, had gone into the library to answer the phone. When she hung up a few minutes later, she felt countless emotions churning deep inside her. The one that surfaced was dread.

She had to find Erik. Hurrying out of the room, she hoped she wasn't too late.

He hadn't been in the ballroom when the phone call came in, so she searched the other downstairs rooms first, with no luck. Trying to appear calm, though her heart was hammering, she decided to try the ballroom again.

She found him in a corner, talking to a group of men. As Julie approached, she heard one of them ask, "Is it true that you are announcing your engagement, old boy?"

The man took Erik's silence as affirmation, and prodded further. "Who's the lucky woman?"

If Erik had been inclined to answer, he didn't have a chance.

"I am." Julie pushed her way into the group and took Erik by the arm. "At least, for one dance. Don't you remember you promised to dance with me?" she asked, looking pleadingly at Erik.

He could hardly refuse her without committing a breach of etiquette that rivaled her own. "Of course. Excuse us, gentlemen."

As soon as they were out of earshot, he said, "What in the world are you doing?"

"Saving your royal behind," Julie said tightly. "Something's come up. We need to talk in private."

Without another word he led her swiftly from the room and ushered her into the library. He closed the heavy double doors behind them and turned to face her. "What is it?"

"You just got an urgent phone call. I couldn't find you."

Erik didn't mince words. "Is it my father?"

Julie shook her head. "Your fian——" she started and then stopped. "Roberta."

"Roberta called? Where is she? Is something wrong?"

"Yes, but not—not an accident or anything like that," she said quickly.

"Then what is it?"

"It's—she's not coming."

"Not coming?" He frowned. "We had been in

agreement that she should be here with me when I make the announcement tonight.''

"That's not all, Your Highness," Julie said. "It's where she is."

"Where is she?"

"Would you like a drink?" she asked, glancing at the liquor cabinet.

Erik would not be distracted. "Where is she?" he repeated.

"On a plane for Las Vegas. She's been trying to reach you, but——"

"Las Vegas? Why the hell is she going there?" Julie hated to be the one to tell him bad news, so she said it as quickly as she could. "To get married——"

"*What?*"

"To a man she said she's always loved but who would never commit to her until tonight when she told him it was over because she was about to be engaged to someone else. But she didn't tell him it was you, and she swears she never breathed a word of it to anyone else, either, and she said to tell you she's sorry but this is for the best, and she wishes you happiness and hopes that you can find it in you to wish her the same." Julie paused and gulped down a breath.

Erik stared at her in silence for a few moments, then said, "Let me make sure I understand you. You're saying that Roberta has called off our engagement."

"Yes," Julie said miserably.

"And she's in the process of eloping with another man."

"Yes." She watched as he struggled with a complex mixture of emotions, much as she had earlier. But his was a very different mixture. Disbelief gave way to shock, shock to anger and anger to cynical control, all within moments.

"I think I'll have that drink now," he said dispassionately. He splashed amber liquid into two glasses and handed one to her.

He took a long swallow. "I've got to hand it to her," he said in a voice of cool amusement. "I never saw it coming."

Julie hadn't, either. A woman would have to have a very good reason to dump a handsome prince—like getting a chance to marry the man she really loved. She took a small sip from her glass and immediately started coughing. Fire shot up from her throat and scorched her sinuses.

He glanced at her. "Are you all right?"

Julie wiped her watery eyes. "Fine," she whispered. She reached for the glass of champagne she had been nursing all evening. It took several swallows until the bubbles obliterated the taste of the bourbon. She sat back in her seat, knowing that any offer of sympathy on her part would not be met with kindly on his part. So she just listened.

"I knew about him, of course, and how desperately she wanted him to fall in love with her. He strung her along mercilessly. When I proposed, she told me she had decided not to continue to waste her life waiting for some romantic dream that's not meant to be."

He refilled his glass. "That's why I thought it would work. I wasn't blinded by emotion and neither was she." With a humorless grin, he added, "At least, not about me."

Julie thought the woman had some nerve agreeing to marry Erik in the first place, without being in love with him. Then again, it seemed that they had both viewed the engagement objectively, not passionately. Not the way she herself could ever view an engagement.

Erik held up his drink. "Well, here's to her happiness, such as she may find it," he said grimly, taking a sip. "And as for me—easy come, easy go."

He finished his drink. It was clear to Julie that he had gotten a lid on his reaction and was ready to move on.

"Now to salvage the situation. That's the tricky part," he said coolly.

Julie wasn't daunted by his cavalier attitude. "I'm the only other person who knows," she said. "I promise I won't tell a soul. All anyone else thinks they know is pure speculation."

"They can speculate as much as they damn please. That's not what concerns me."

Suddenly Julie realized what he was talking about. The rumor of Erik's engagement had spread farther than to the crowd waiting in the ballroom. "Your father," she whispered.

"I know," he said soberly, meeting her concerned look with one of his own.

"I hate to say it, but you really got the king's hopes up. It was obvious when I spoke to him on the phone earlier." She looked at the clock. "It's almost midnight. What are you going to do?"

He sat down at the desk and linked his hands behind his neck. "I'm going to think of something," he said simply.

"I'll help you any way I can," she offered. "Is there anything you would like me to do?"

"Yes. Go back out there. If you need to, stall the crowd," he said.

"What if your father calls?"

"Stall him, too."

"All right." At the door Julie turned and looked back at him. "I just hope you're better at thinking than I am at stalling."

Out in the hall she leaned back against the library door for a moment, trying to regain her composure. After taking the call, she couldn't help hurting for Erik. But she felt better now, after seeing how he had taken the news of his fiancée's elopement. His reaction had confirmed her earlier suspicion that he hadn't been in love with the woman. He was more upset at being jilted than at losing her.

Erik, as always, was very much in control. He would think of something.

Damn. He couldn't think of *anything*.

Erik paced back and forth and swore the vilest swears he knew in every language he knew, but it didn't help.

What a *fool* he had been.

He had hidden it pretty well in front of Julie, but the news of Roberta's betrayal had cut like a knife. There was nothing she could have done that went more against Erik's code of honor than to go back on her word. The only consolation he could find, and it was meager, was that in jilting him, Roberta had taught him a wonderful lesson: when it comes to duty, never trust a woman.

The problem was there was one woman he had no choice but to trust. Julie. Like it or not, she knew everything. And that would either make her his worst enemy or his best ally.

He wished he knew which.

One thing was sure. There was no time to waste brooding. He had made a foolish mistake, and now it was time to pay up. He figured he had three choices.

One choice was to fabricate an announcement of some sort, and somehow brazen his way through it.

The second was to ignore the rumors and simply not make any announcement, and somehow brazen his way through that.

Then there was the third. Erik stared out of the barred library window, across the inky blackness of the ocean far below. He wondered if the king were looking out of his hospital window, across that same ocean, toward their beloved homeland.

As for the third choice, he wasn't sure he could brazen his way through that one at all. Which was really too damned bad. Because it was the only real choice he had.

Relief swept through Julie when she saw Erik enter the ballroom. She envied him his composure. She wondered if that was a hallmark of royalty or a gift passed down from his intrepid Viking ancestors. At any rate he didn't look like a man whose future had just been pulled out from under him.

His eyes met hers, and he gave her a barely perceptible nod. Cool, controlled, he had apparently figured out a way to deal with this challenge. He started across the room. As a dutiful host, he talked briefly with several different groups that stopped him on the way. She watched as he detached a matched pair of blond high-fashion models from his arms, listening with no more than required politeness. But even when he wasn't looking her way, Julie could tell that his attention was focused on her.

Eventually he reached her.

"You thought of something?" she asked softly.

He said nothing, but his expression made it clear that he had. Not that it was easy to detect his smile; Julie noticed it more in his brown eyes than on his lips. But that tiny twinkle deep in their depths worked on her like magic, shot her through with a cascade of tingles that had nothing to do with the glass of champagne she had finally finished, and was far more intoxicating.

"Is…is there anything you would like me to do, Your Highness?" she asked.

"Yes." The sound of his voice, though low and formal as ever, did not dispel the momentary magic, but enhanced it. "Dance with me."

He ushered her through the crowd to the dance floor and turned to face her, his brown eyes burning amber in the light from the crystal chandelier overhead. He offered her his hand, and she put hers in it. Almost shyly she rested the other on his shoulder. As he put his arm around her waist, she had to fight the impulse to close the distance between their bodies that formality dictated.

They danced one slow revolution around the floor. While he maneuvered a corner, he tightened his arm around her, ever so slightly drawing her body closer to his.

Julie closed her eyes, taking silent pleasure in the things he was making her feel. Once again she was at a royal ball, at a castle, dancing with a handsome prince. The last time she had been a naive teenager, convinced that they were destined for happily-ever-after with each other. But Erik was no fairy-tale prince. He was a real man, and very much a man, and something in him, something deep and masculine, called to her. Had he been a pauper, she still would have responded to that something she felt tugging at her.

He broke into her thoughts. "Now that we're alone, here's what I've decided," he said in a low voice.

About what? Julie wondered to herself. She was lost in his encircling arms, held captive in a teasing embrace where their bodies just touched, whispering against each other in time to the music. Couldn't he feel it? Obviously not. If he felt it as powerfully as she did, he would...what? Fall to his knees, pledging his undying love and begging her to be his bride? Get real, Julie, she told herself. He wasn't engaged anymore, but he was just as out of reach for her.

"Julie?".

Garnering her powers of concentration, Julie glanced at her watch. Ten minutes until midnight. "Are you going to make an announcement, Your Highness?"

"Yes."

"What are you going to announce?"

"My engagement."

She gave him a worried look. "Are you sure about that? I mean, isn't having someone to be your fiancée sort of a standard requirement for announcing an engagement?"

"I want you to be my fiancée."

Julie suddenly stopped dancing, forcing him to a standstill with her. Expecting them to have moved along with the flow, several other couples jostled into them before they, too, stopped.

Had she heard the words, or conjured them out of her imagination? "I beg your pardon," she said weakly. "I-I'm afraid I didn't hear you correctly."

"I'm certain that you did," Erik answered. Her reaction had confirmed that.

"You're asking me to…" She let her voice trail off, suddenly aware that they were the center of a growing amount of attention. Even her whisper sounded loud in the sudden silence of the ballroom.

The musicians, seeing that the prince had stopped dancing, had brought their music to a ragged halt. Cursing the inconvenient lack of privacy, Erik signaled the conductor to continue the music. When she did, Erik pulled Julie through the French doors, out to the side lawn.

He made sure they were alone before he spoke. "You asked if you could help with my problem," he said. "Well, you can do more than that. You can be my—"

"Fiancée?" she said, disbelieving.

"Solution," he finished.

Julie faced the ocean and took several deep, cleansing breaths. She didn't quite know what Erik was proposing. But she knew for sure that he wasn't proposing marriage.

"Your Highness," she said. "Would you mind explaining to me just what in the world you are talking about?"

Erik's words were terse. "In five minutes I'm supposed to be announcing my engagement. Not only does everyone in that crowded ballroom expect it, but a man lying in a hospital bed in Boston does, too."

"I know."

"Roberta is out of the picture," he went on. "But no one but you knew about her, anyway. So I can still make the announcement. All I need is a—" he paused, choosing the best word "—partner."

Julie rested her hand against her chest. "Me?"

"You." She was the perfect choice. Outwardly she

was regal and poised and possessed the kind of so-phisticated charm which made her a logical choice for a prince's bride. The style and efficiency with which she had executed the planning of this ball bore witness to the world that she could perform the duties that would be expected of the future queen of Isle Anders. She could handle the role of fake fiancée, he was sure of it. Best of all, she was not only loyal to the king, her real affection for him was obvious in her concern over his health—and Erik hoped this would motivate her.

"Why *me?*"

"You offered to help," Erik pointed out. And she knew everything, anyway, so it made sense to make her part of his plan. If he sweetened the pot a little for her, maybe she wouldn't betray his trust.

Julie interrupted his thoughts. "I did offer to help, but I don't—" she began.

"I'm not talking about you being my real fiancée, naturally." After what happened with Roberta, Erik knew that would be too risky.

"Naturally," Julie echoed dryly. What kind of fool would think that? *She* was not that kind of fool, not anymore.

Erik went on. "I just want you to pose as my fiancée, so the king can put his worries to rest." He swore mildly under his breath. "Believe me, I don't like this idea any more than you do, but at this point I'm afraid it may be the only way to help him recover and resume rule of the kingdom. You want that, too, don't you?"

It went without saying. "Of course, but—"

"Think of it as a promotion," Erik said persuasively.

"I don't want a promotion. I love my job."

"You can still have it. This will be a temporary position."

"Obviously," Julie said evenly. "But when will it end?"

"That depends on the king's recovery," Erik said. His expression hardened. "But one thing is for sure."

"Yes?"

"If you agree to do this, you also agree that I will be the one to end it."

Julie didn't have to be as in tune with him as she was to know that he didn't want to be jilted again, even by a pretend fiancée. His vulnerability did her in, even more than her fear for the king's health.

"Julie, time is running out. What is your answer?"

In the split second that followed, he could tell that she was making a quick review of the options. Even the brilliance of her sapphire blue eyes couldn't mask the intelligence that lay behind them. Those eyes, framed by spiky dark lashes, focused on him, wide and unblinking, as she spoke.

"Yes," she said.

He searched her face. "You'll do it?"

She nodded.

"And you agree with the conditions?"

She gave him a faint smile. "It ain't over till you say it's over," she said lightly, noticing that her agreement didn't dispel his tension.

"Now, what would you like in return?" he asked.

"Me? I don't want anything."

"I insist," he said. "A new car, a vacation——"

"Don't be ridiculous!"

"A raise, a bonus. You name it."

"Your Highness, there is no need to insult me by

offering monetary incentive. I'm doing this for the sake of the king."

"I know that. But this is for your sake." And his own. He wanted there to be something in it for her, something real, that would cement her loyalty. "I'm asking a lot of you," he reasoned. "It only seems fair that you ask something of me."

Julie glanced at her watch. "One minute to midnight. We'd better get inside."

Reluctantly Erik agreed. The details would have to wait. "Time to get to work," he said.

He was all business as he escorted her back into the ballroom. Not surprisingly, Julie thought. Erik was taking a big personal risk for the sake of his father and the kingdom. But he was a man of duty, and right now duty meant making this plan work. Making her his partner. But it was plain to Julie that he didn't really trust her. He simply had no other choice.

Just as she'd had no choice but to say yes.

As they entered the ballroom, the whole place went dark. Julie took Erik's arm, and he led her onto the platform in front of the orchestra. She felt him tense up as he murmured in her ear, "This is it, sweetheart."

His whispered endearment sent a raw shiver through her.

To his surprise, she gave his hand a squeeze that was oddly reassuring.

At that moment the spotlight flared on dramatically, catching the look that passed between them, igniting a murmur among the onlookers. As fire licks through dry brush, speculation spread throughout the room, almost visibly transforming the places it touched.

Erik broke off the gaze first. He offered Julie his arm, and walked with her to the center of the stage.

She tried to absorb some of his calm assurance as he stood at her elbow facing the crowd, solid, dignified.

His voice was resonant in the big room. ''Ladies and gentlemen of many lands, my honored guests, my countrymen and women and—,'' he glanced at the camera ''—Your Majesty, King Ivar of Isle Anders.''

He paused, gave a slight bow and announced formally, ''It is a great honor to present to you my betrothed, Miss Julie Britton.''

Julie gulped and inclined her head, as he had done, but she feared that all resemblance to his regal bearing faded there.

The crowd made no immediate reaction, but waited, expectantly.

Erik wondered what it was that everyone seemed to expect from him. He looked down at Julie. ''What are they waiting for?'' he asked so softly that only she could hear.

She gave him a smile so sweet it made something in him ache. ''I think they're waiting for us to seal the deal,'' she said, almost apologetically. When he still looked puzzled, she added, ''With a kiss.''

A *kiss*. He really hadn't thought about that, but it was clear that there was no way around it. He gathered her into his arms. To those watching it would look like they were exchanging lovers' vows.

''It's still not a deal,'' he whispered in her ear. ''Not really. Not until you tell me what you want from me.''

Julie felt a shudder go through her and knew that somewhere deep inside, the hopes that she had thought were dead and buried were rising out of their grave, reckless, indomitable. There was only one thing she wanted from him, now or ever, and it was the last thing he would ever be able to give her.

"Julie," he persisted. "What do you want me to do?"

He felt a rush of masculine anticipation as her hands settled on his lapels. Slowly she leaned toward him, her lips hovering tantalizingly just below his. Her eyes dropped closed just before she whispered a single word request.

"Believe."

Before her breath had cooled, his lips met hers, and the word spoken so softly he thought he must have imagined it became lost in the reality of a kiss as sweet and warm as new honey. Ah, but her lips were ripe and moist, firm where he wanted them to be firm, yielding where he wanted them to be yielding. He covered her mouth with his and ran his tongue along her lips, slowly. They were full, they were smooth, and, wonder of sweet wonders, they eased apart for him.

That was enough to rally Erik's scattered senses, and not a moment too soon. He ended the kiss with a very proper pucker. What had come over him? He had no right to involve tongues in this kiss. This wasn't a real engagement kiss, it was the kiss of conspirators. Luckily, he had remembered that before he got carried away.

He took a step back. The applause that had begun with the kiss rose to a thunderous pitch, filling the massive room from wall to wall, all the way to the ceiling. The crowd believed. Erik's job was done. He settled his arm around Julie's shoulders and led her out through one of the stone archways at the side of the ballroom.

It was over.

Chapter Three

Cool air from an open door whispered along the stone walls of the passageway where they walked. Apparently, security lived up to its reputation. No one followed them from the ballroom.

Erik had dropped his arm from Julie's shoulder as soon as they had made good their exit. "I think that went even better than we could have hoped," he said evenly.

Julie rolled her eyes, but refrained from voicing her disagreement. Her first kiss from Erik had been a huge disappointment. It was her own fault, she supposed, after all those years of anticipation. Still, even under the strange circumstances, she felt he could have done better than seem actually *reluctant* to kiss her.

He gave her a sideways glance. "I'm sorry about the kiss."

"You should be," she snapped, for the sake of her bruised ego. The kiss had started off slow, until she had felt the warm glide of his tongue. Then, when she had tried to encourage him by parting her lips, he'd had the nerve to coolly break off the contact!

"It was...awkward," he said in agreement. In agreeing to pose as his fiancée, Julie obviously hadn't bargained on being forced into physical intimacy with him.

What had made it awkward for him, however, was the unaccustomed feeling of having to exercise restraint. He never usually had any trouble controlling his passion. Except with her.

"Let's just forget about it," she said.

Easy for her to say. Right now he was still battling the urge to back her up against the nearest wall and continue the kiss right where they had left off.

They came to the back staircase. Naturally he let her go first, which gave him an enticing, eye-level view of her derriere on the way up the narrow flight of stairs. As a distraction, he made a mental list of all the reasons he had chosen her as his partner. Nowhere on that list was the fact that he was attracted to her. No, sir.

His reasons were perfectly logical. She was simply the best woman for the job, and he had no reason to feel guilty about getting her into this. She was a full-grown, independent woman, freely capable of making her own choices. She had gone along with his plan of her own free will, for reasons of her own. He conjectured that her loyalty to the king had played as big a part in her decision as it had in his choosing her.

When they got to the top of the stairs he walked her down the hall, keeping a careful distance between them.

"We have a lot more details to discuss," he said. "The details will wait. I'm going to bed." She opened the door to the bedroom that gave access to her tower room.

The bed was strewn with hastily shed men's clothing.

Erik stared at her in disbelief. "I never asked, but I assumed you were single and unattached."

"I am!"

"Then whose clothes are these?"

"I was just going to ask you that."

They went into the room. Erik saw a suitcase in one corner. He looked at it and swore.

"This is Whit's stuff," he said.

Julie frowned. "But the king told me he was sending Prince Whit back to Isle Anders."

"Looks like my brother couldn't resist taking a slight detour."

"He never was one to miss a good party."

Erik started stuffing clothes into the suitcase. "He probably came in while we were outside. No doubt he heard the announcement."

He didn't have to say anything more for Julie to know that he was worried about whether his brother had bought it. She was worried about the same thing. If Whit suspected, and said anything to the king....

"What are you doing?" she asked, as Erik snapped the suitcase shut.

He gave her the kind of look that people exiting UFOs probably got. "What kind of fiancé would I be if I would let my brother sleep in the room adjoining yours?"

She had to admit, he had a point there. "Luckily I had those two other bedrooms made up for you," Julie pointed out. "You and Whit can each have one."

He gave her another one of those looks. "Whit can have them both."

"Why?"

He tried to think of a delicate way to word it. "Julie, my brother knows me rather well. Well enough to know where I'd sleep, if I had a fiancée."

Julie gulped at that intimate thought.

Erik noticed. "It goes without saying that I will sleep down here in this bed," he said, wanting to reassure her. "As long as we're both behind the same closed door, we can let Whit's imagination take care of the rest."

Julie winced at yet another blow that had made a direct hit on her ego. Apparently he was not worried that her living literally on top of him would prove a temptation.

He picked up the suitcase and headed out to switch rooms. In the doorway he paused and looked back at her pained expression. "Go on up to your room in the tower, princess," he said softly. "I promise you'll be safe from me."

Julie went through the open archway in the corner of the room and up the stone steps of the spiral staircase beyond. At the top was the room that had been hers for the past year. Its curved walls outlined a perfect circle. Windows, also curved, faced out in every direction, encompassing views of the town, the grounds and of course the ocean. It was at the top of the tower, and she had chosen it because it was unique, it was romantic, and it had been Erik's.

Gazing out a window of her remote room, she thought about what Erik had said. He was a man who could be utterly depended upon to stick to his promises.

Still, she wondered if there were anywhere in the world where she would be safe from Erik Anders.

At daybreak Julie woke. She pulled on a T-shirt and shorts and went quietly down the spiral stairs. To her surprise, Erik's bed was empty and made up. He might have changed his mind about sleeping there, after all.

She made for the bathroom, stretching the kinks out of her still-tired muscles as she went. Washing up woke her fully. She brushed her teeth and put her hair in a quick braid.

Padding barefoot down the big stone stairway, she saw no one, which was fine with her. And not too surprising. It was way too early for breakfast, especially the night after a ball. Everyone must still be asleep. As for her, she was out of there.

Noiselessly she slipped out the front door. Two steps from her car she realized she had forgotten her keys. She didn't even pause before starting to walk down the road to Anders Point. It was a gorgeous June morning, and the dirt road was early-morning cool on her bare feet. She took a deep breath of the fresh, coastal Maine air. Birds played in and out of the cliffs on her left, in the weeds on her right. All was right with the world.

Except in her little corner of it.

She had heard once that you should be careful what you wish for, because it might come true. Well, her long-ago wish to marry Prince Erik had sure taken a bizarre twist. Last night she had been toasted as the prince's future bride; but, quite the opposite of how it appeared to the world, it was obvious to her that she was as far from actually becoming his bride as any woman on the planet. Farther.

The whole pretend engagement idea seemed so ridiculous in the daylight. How had she and Erik ever thought they'd get away with it? And if King Ivar found out they were trying to fool him, it would be worse than if Erik had never gotten engaged at all. The *best* that could happen would be that Julie would lose the job she loved and her friendship with the king.

She didn't want to think about the worst.

King Ivar simply couldn't find out, and neither could anyone else, including Whit. It was absurd. Here Julie was, pretending to be engaged, and she couldn't even tell her best friends the true story.

The true story was that she was a romantic fool who had put herself in a foolish position. At the ball she had felt that same silly spark again—the one that, again, Erik hadn't. And then there was that insulting kiss. It was worse than embarrassing. At least spending time with the prince and seeing his indifference to her would be a surefire way to cure whatever vestiges remained of her ridiculous girlhood infatuation.

Halfway to town she saw a car cruising up the castle road in her direction, churning up a cloud of dust that dispersed in the breeze from the ocean. It was Drew, alone—Lexi must have spent the night with a friend.

In moments Drew pulled over next to her. "I thought that was you," she said as Julie got in beside her.

"Am I glad to see you," Julie said. "I could use a cup of Annah's coffee, the sooner the better."

"You look it," Drew said, glancing over at her while she turned the car around. "Cinderella after the ball. So how was it, anyway?"

"Not bad."

"You didn't fall in love, did you?"

Julie had been dreading this, but she decided just to

go ahead and get it over with. "Worse," she said with a wry smile. "I got engaged."

The car veered abruptly, its two right tires laboring along the rut at the side of the road. With a jerk of the steering wheel, Drew swerved back onto the road. "You *what?*" she demanded, her tone incredulous.

"Got engaged," Julie repeated.

Apparently shocked into silence, Drew drove slowly down the hill. The castle road led to only one place, and that was to the town of Anders Point, referred to by locals simply as "the Point." Located along the same spit of land that jutted out into the Atlantic as the castle, the town was so far off the beaten track that its spectacular view was enjoyed mostly by residents. In a few minutes Drew pulled over and parked in front of Annah's.

They got out of the car, Drew visibly wrestling with Julie's revelation. Inside, Annah was behind the coffee counter, getting ready for a busy morning.

"You are not going to believe what happened to Julie at that ball last night," Drew said, her tone still incredulous. "She got *engaged.*"

Annah stopped working to look closely at Julie. "No, she didn't," she said decisively.

"She says she did," Drew argued.

Annah looked at Julie again. "Impossible," she declared. "She's not in love."

Of course she wasn't, Julie thought. Love had nothing to do with the engagement! Annah could spot true love a mile away, so it was no surprise that she could spot its absence right under her nose. Julie decided to sidestep the love issue and focus on the engagement. "*Impossible?*" she said with a laugh. "Thanks a lot, Annah! Whatever happened to *congratulations?*"

"You're really engaged? I'm so sorry, Julie!" Annah said, horrified. "I thought Drew was joking, because my true love instinct has always been on target before. But, wow! What a way to be wrong!" She leaned over the counter and gave Julie a hard hug. "I take it you found Mr. Right at the ball?"

"Not Mr. Right. Prince Right," Drew corrected. She was looking at the headline of the morning paper, which she had picked up from the doorstep.

"Talk about romantic!" Annah said, apparently willing to abandon all her doubts, which made Julie feel like a skunk. "You go to a ball, fall in love with a prince——"

Drew rolled her eyes. "Like she's never done *that* before."

"Something no one else needs to know," Julie warned. Especially the prince in question.

Annah, handing them each a cup of coffee, ignored the byplay. "You fall in love with Prince Erik, who offers you his hand in marriage, thereby depriving the world of one of the Anders brothers, its most eligible bachelors."

"Whit, *eligible?*" Drew said scornfully. "He is the world's most notorious playboy, as anyone who has ever gone into a supermarket knows. He's on the cover of those tabloids with a different woman every week."

"But they call Whit the Prince of Hearts," Annah reminded her.

"Because he breaks them," Drew pointed out. She shrugged. "So he's put the panty hose of half the world's population in a twist. I fail to see how that makes him husband material."

Julie understood her friend's cynicism. Drew had gotten pregnant while Julie was away at college and had never told her who the father was—presumably someone she had met while attending the local community college. But Drew had admitted that he had left her to play the field. To her credit, she had held her head high and gone on to raise Lexi without the help of him or any man. If anyone had a right to be down on a playboy type, even one who used to be their friend, it was Drew.

Annah conceded the point and changed the subject. "Well, as far as Julie is concerned, Prince Erik is the only one who needs to be husband material," she said. "Now all that's left is for them to get married and live happily ever after."

"I don't see how that could possibly happen," said Drew pragmatically. "I mean, this is so unbelievably sudden that—"

Annah interrupted her. "Didn't you ever hear of people falling suddenly, madly in love?"

"At least once before," Drew pointed out dryly.

"Drew!" Annah said, exasperated. She turned to Julie. "So, when do we get to congratulate the groom-to-be?"

In the silence that followed, there came a noise from the front door. "How about now?" Erik said as he stepped inside.

Julie felt all her blood whoosh to her feet, then slowly pump back. She wondered how much of the conversation he had heard through the screen door. Not the part about loving him, she hoped—although she didn't see how he could have missed it.

"Wh-what are you doing here?" she blurted out.

"Getting a cup of what I hear is the best coffee on the Point," he said, taking a seat at the counter beside her.

Struggling for composure, Julie turned to her friends. Their reactions were predictable: Annah's eyes had widened with interest; Drew's had narrowed with skepticism. Julie wasn't sure which was worse.

Dressed in a college T-shirt, shorts and running shoes, Erik looked like the guy next door. But he took control of the situation like the would-be king he was. He shook hands with Drew, whom he remembered. Then he introduced himself to Annah, who congratulated him and gave him a friendly hug.

"You couldn't have made a better choice for a princess," Annah told him warmly, pouring him a cup of coffee.

Princess, ha, Julie thought. She wasn't going to be Erik's bride; this was nothing but a temp job to him. As quickly as she could, she drained her coffee cup. Annah's regular customers would start showing up soon.

"Well, it's been fun, but I guess we'd better be going," she said, looking pointedly at Erik. Then she said to Drew and Annah, "If either of you need me, you know where I'll be. See you later." She pulled Erik out the door behind her, but not without noticing the looks of doubt and concern on the faces of her two friends.

"Where are you parked?" he asked her when they got outside.

"At the castle."

He cast her a questioning glance.

"I locked myself out this morning," she explained.

"Must have been all the excitement," he murmured.

"I doubt that. I lock myself out regularly," she said, shrugging. "So, as usual, I walked here."

He glanced down. "Barefoot?"

"Yes," she said with a puzzled look. "It's not that far. Why not?"

Because it didn't fit in with the image he had of her, Erik thought as he excused himself to get the car he had leased for his stay in America. A woman who had planned a royal ball as efficiently as she had, forgetting her keys on a regular basis? A woman whom he had chosen to pose as his future queen, partly because of her elegance and sophistication, walking two miles on a dirt road, barefoot?

And those weren't the only things making him uneasy. In her cutoff jeans and white T-shirt, her freckled nose and casual braid, she looked exactly like a sweet, homespun girl. As she had sounded, when chatting with her friends—close friends, if they were any judge. That wasn't the kind of woman he was looking for at all. His mother had been just such a simple girl from Anders Point, abundant with homespun charm, delighted with the joy she found in the world that surrounded her, deeply in love with her husband and children—and she had left a huge, aching void in their lives after she was gone.

Here in the streets of her beloved hometown, Erik felt the familiar bite of an old, half-healed wound. When his mother died, he had been young enough to be devastated, but old enough to think he shouldn't be. Not knowing what to do with the pain, he had buried it deep. What's more, he had seen firsthand the emotional hell his father had gone through at losing the wife he had loved so deeply. The king's suffering had been solitary, silent, profound. He had immersed himself in his duties—and had never been the same since.

Neither had Erik, but he had learned a valuable lesson: love was too big a risk, too arbitrary in its power.

If you weren't careful, it would swallow you up and spit you out. He steered clear of women like his mother, the kind of woman you could fall in love with.

Give someone your heart, and you find one day that they're gone. Duty, on the other hand, made you strong, not vulnerable. A marriage for duty with a different kind of woman would be safe and predictable.

Just as this fake engagement was supposed to be. But Erik didn't quite seem safe, because Julie didn't quite seem predictable. Who was the real Julie Britton, anyway? The demure sophisticate of last night, or the tousled barefoot beauty of this morning?

Casting his thoughts backward, he feared that the pendulum was swinging toward the latter. He remembered her as she had appeared at the ball. Her demeanor had been naturally unselfconscious, not because she had been schooled to appear unaware of her charm like most of the women who traveled in such circles. Their beauty—all that money could buy—couldn't compare to her brilliant smile, which had lit up the stale, stuffy crowd of the ballroom more than the crystal chandeliers that hung from its ceilings. She had outshone every other woman in the room, despite their glitz and glitter, precisely because her glow was so very, very real.

And so very sexy. He pulled over to the curb where she stood waiting and got out of the car. Opening the passenger door for her, he watched her fold her long legs into the low-slung two-seater. He kept his manner casual, but underneath he was working to keep a lid on a boiling reservoir of unreleased tension. It had started with that kiss last night at the ball. He'd suffered an uncharacteristically restless night. Even a five-mile run at dawn had brought him no relief.

Returning to the castle to find Julie gone hadn't improved his frame of mind one damn bit more than finding her here in town involved in a cozy chat with her girlfriends.

"You were in a hurry to leave," he observed as he got into the driver's seat beside her.

"Didn't you want to?" Julie said, raising one eyebrow knowingly. "Isn't that why you came chasing after me?"

Chasing her? He felt like quieting that impertinent mouth of hers with a long, slow kiss. Instead he called on his reserves of control. "I was surprised to find you gone when I got back to the castle after my run," he said evenly. But in truth he'd half expected her to leave him—especially after how upset she'd been about the kiss last night.

"You weren't planning on keeping me locked away in the tower, were you, Your Highness?"

"Not at all. You can run out on me anytime you like," he observed dryly, starting the car and pulling away from the curb.

Julie thought she heard something more in his words than he might have meant to express and wondered if she had underestimated the effect the jilt had on him. Her voice softened. "I'm not running," she assured him. "I had to tell my friends about our…engagement, before they read about it in the paper."

"I had hoped that we would talk this morning and get our story straight, before either of us went out in public," he said. "What did you tell your friends?"

Not the truth, Julie thought miserably. "As little as I could," she admitted.

"I heard mention of the word *love*."

Julie shrugged noncommittally. "It's the usual reason people get engaged."

He thought about that. "I guess the simpler the story, the better."

"I guess so."

"And the easier to remember."

"Yes."

"And we need a good explanation, given how sudden the announcement was."

"The announcement would have been sudden for you and Roberta, too," Julie reminded him.

Erik didn't want to talk about Roberta. "That was different," he said flatly. "It was well-known that she and I had dated for years."

"Mmm. That won't work for us."

He met her eyes. "So what's our story? We fell suddenly, madly in love?"

"I hear it happens," Julie said, forcing a casual shrug. It had happened to her, once.

"Hard to believe," he said cynically, though feeling odd at remembering that he himself had almost fallen, once. "But if that's the story that will make this engagement seem legit, let's go with it."

He spoke with clinical detachment. Despite herself, that hurt Julie. "It's not easy making it work in front of your two best friends, you know," she warned. "I'd like to see you pull it off, Your Highness."

"You're about to get half your wish," he said as he drove past the entrance to the castle grounds. "My brother is still inside."

He parked by the kitchen entrance and Julie was surprised to see that, besides hers, there were no other cars there. "What happened to Gustave and the rest of the staff?'' she asked. ''They weren't supposed to leave until tonight.''

''I paid them a bonus to clean up and clear out before I went running this morning,'' he said. Erik liked his privacy, and now he had an additional reason for wanting it. With them supposed to be engaged, he didn't want any hired help underfoot in the castle, especially anyone who might hear too much and say too much. He had told Gustave that he wanted to be alone with Julie, sure that that information would be passed along to his father.

Julie waited while he opened the door, correctly guessing the line of his thinking. ''That means you and I will be all alone here at the castle—''

''Only after I leave,'' said a voice from inside. ''So out of pity for my poor, broken heart, please try to keep your hands off each other.''

Walking into the kitchen, Julie broke into a smile. ''Whit!'' she said.

He was sitting behind a cup of coffee at the big, wooden trestle table, his patented heart-stopping smile a crooked slash in his unshaven face.

''Julie,'' he said, standing up and spreading his arms wide. She went over to him and was instantly enveloped in a big, warm hug.

''I take it you heard the news,'' Erik said.

''I arrived at the ball just in time for your announcement, big brother,'' Whit said, releasing Julie. ''But I'm having a hard time convincing myself it's true.''

''Why is that?'' Erik asked, his eyes both wary and challenging.

Whit grinned. ''Because I was engaged to her first.''

Julie laughed in relief. ''We were eight years old and

it lasted a day and a half," she told Erik. "Then I found out he had already asked Drew to marry him."

"True, but she turned me down," Whit pointed out.

"Smart girl," Julie retorted. She hadn't seen Whit since before he had gone to college, when his reputation with the ladies had first come to the attention of the media. But the boy she had known had been destined to break hearts. All grown up, he was textbook handsome, with dark hair that fell to his shoulders in luxuriant waves, teasing blue eyes and that irrepressible smile. She had always liked Whit; but he was not the prince she had once fallen in love with and was pretending to be in love with now.

Whit turned to his brother. "If you had chosen anyone else, I would have suspected you of doing this just to appease Dad. But given that it's Julie—well, congratulations," he said, giving him a hard hug. "Any man this woman loves is one lucky bastard." He winked at Julie. "It was about time you figured that out, Erik, given that she always—"

Her childhood friends, Julie decided, had the most unfortunate ability to recall her past mistakes with stunning clarity. Before Whit could tell his brother about her crush on him in mortifying detail, Julie changed the subject. "Remember what Drew and I used to call you?"

"Yeah, I know. And once a flirt, always a flirt," Whit said. "No reason to change, now that my big brother is going to get married and sire himself a castle full of heirs." He gave Erik a knowing grin.

Julie didn't dare look at Erik, but she was sure even he couldn't miss the blush that warmed her cheeks. She hurried to change the subject yet again. "Aren't you going to ask me about Drew?" she said to Whit.

"Sure," he answered vaguely. "How is she?"

"Why don't you find out for yourself while you're in town?" Julie suggested. "She still lives right down the road, in her grandmother's house."

"Really?" he said, looking up sharply. "I thought she was going to sell that house and move away from the Point after her grandmother died."

Julie looked at him curiously. "You knew that her grandmother had died?" As far as she was aware, he hadn't been in Anders Point since the last ball, when they were both sixteen. Drew's grandmother had still been alive then; had in fact refused to let Drew attend the ball.

His only answer was a slight shrug. Then he picked up a package from the table and handed it to Erik. "This was just delivered for you."

"Ah. I wasn't expecting it so soon," Erik said. He started opening it.

"What is it?" Whit asked.

"A little something I asked our friend Lucas to send." He pulled out a small, velvet-covered box.

"You mean Prince Lucas, from the Constellation Isles?" Julie asked, peering over his shoulder. "The one who needs to find a bride or else lose his crown?"

"Yes, poor guy," Whit said, then quickly added, "Whoops, sorry. No offense, Julie."

"None taken," Julie said smoothly. She, after all, had no intention of being Erik's *bride*.

"Lucas is a good buddy of ours," Whit added. To Erik he said, "Is that what I think it is?"

"Yes." Erik opened the lid of the box and looked inside.

"What?" Julie asked.

"Your engagement ring," Whit told her. "The Constellation Isles are renowned for jewelry making. Although I'm sure Erik is planning to wait for a more private and romantic moment to give that to you."

"Naturally," Erik said, snapping the box closed.

"Let's go, Julie."

"Is he always this bossy?" she asked Whit. His laughter followed them out of the room.

When they reached the bottom of the main staircase, Erik stopped. "Here," he said, tossing the velvet box to her. "You'd better wear this."

She missed catching it, and it fell to the floor. Bending down to pick it up gave her a chance to hide the unexpected disappointment that she was sure must be written all over her face.

What did you expect, Julie girl? she chided herself. *Romantic?* You should be glad you at least got *private.* She was fairly sure that if Whit hadn't said something, Erik would have unceremoniously handed her the box right there in the kitchen.

She had stuffed the box safely in her pocket when Whit came after them.

"I forgot to tell you," he said. "Dad called this morning while you were gone."

Halfway up the stairs, Erik froze. "Really?" he asked, his voice casual. "What did he say?"

"You mean after he gave me hell for being here when I'm supposed to be on Isle Anders?"

"I meant about my announcement."

"Your announcement was why I came," Whit said, playfully keeping Erik in suspense. "After hearing the rumor, I thought I'd better come find out for myself if it was true."

Erik was clearly in danger of losing even his considerable patience. "What did he say?" he asked again.

Whit grinned. "You know the king, Erik. He doesn't give much away. But he said it did his heart good to know that you're engaged."

Erik let out a pent-up breath, then glanced over at Julie. She flashed him a smile of genuine relief. She must appreciate, as he did, that they were over the last big hurdle. Now it was a matter of holing up here in the castle, biding their time until the king got well.

"One more thing, Erik," Whit said, from below.

"Yes?"

"The king said he is very much looking forward to a visit from you and his future daughter-in-law."

Chapter Four

It wasn't working.

Julie knew that as well as she knew that she and Erik *had* to make their fake engagement work.

The miles to Boston sped by, bringing them closer to their visit with King Ivar. Erik sat on one side of the royal jet, talking shop with Whit, who would be flying to Isle Anders from Boston. Erik seemed completely engrossed in the stack of papers that sat between him and his brother. That left Julie to figure out what was wrong.

Their plan had started off fine at the ball. It was obvious from the applause as well as from the eyewitness accounts in the newspaper the next day. No one watching had noticed the hesitation and tentativeness that Julie herself had registered with heart-stopping intensity. The kiss must have looked much better than it had felt.

After that, though, it was all downhill. Awkward was the best way she could describe their performance in front of Drew and Annah. And in front of Whit. If they didn't do better, they were going to crash and burn right under the king's nose.

But why? After they had left Whit yesterday morning, they had spent the day holed up together behind a closed door. It must have looked like they had spent the whole day in each other's arms. Of course, nothing could have been farther from the truth. Erik had stayed in his room, she in her tower. But Whit didn't know that.

Still, this morning, when Erik and Julie had taken their seats in the plane, Whit had given them a funny look. And she could still see the looks on Drew's and Annah's faces when she and Erik had left the coffee shop the day before. What was it?

Unconcerned, Erik was passing papers over to Whit. Julie couldn't help but notice that her fiancé looked absolutely scrumptious in the glasses he wore for reading. "This is the information about the dispute over the international fishing waters around Isle Anders," he was saying to his brother. "The situation has stabilized, and I don't expect any new developments before fall. As for the tourist commission, the new agenda..."

Julie found their conversation interesting. As a leader, King Ivar had a reputation for being both fair and astute, and it was obvious that Erik was likeminded. So was Whit, though that would have surprised the world at large, given his playboy image. It was no wonder to Julie that study after study found that the population of Isle Anders enjoyed a high standard of living, literacy rate and degree of citizen satisfaction—although such findings always confounded the experts.

Yes, the island was a monarchy, but it was a constitutional monarchy; the Anders family ruled both by tradition and by the people's choice. The system ended up working better than some democracies, because the people had a direct say in their government. Quite literally, they had the ear of the king, who knew nearly all of them personally. The monarchy stayed because, overwhelmingly, the people wanted it to: because it was a centuries-old tradition, because it was a boon to the island's tourism industry, because the independent wealth of the ruling family meant that hard-earned money paid in taxes wasn't squandered on the frivolous excesses of royalty, and because the Anders family had served Isle Anders so well, both at home and abroad.

As far as Julie knew, it was a system unique in the world. Even a staunchly independent Mainer like her had to admire it and the family that made it work. They worked hard and loved the land they served. She wasn't the only one praying for the king's recovery. The entire population of Isle Anders waited with bated breath for his return to his homeland. She gulped when she thought of the responsibility she had taken on in agreeing to this plan of Erik's.

When the jet landed, a limousine was waiting to take Julie and Erik to the hospital. Julie hugged Whit goodbye, finding his friendly warmth gave her a badly needed boost before going to see the king. It was a welcome contrast to his brother's aloofness.

All during the limo ride, Erik was on the phone. Not until they were dropped off in front of the hospital did she have a chance to share her concerns with him, before they had to appear together in front of the king.

"Erik, we need to talk."

"Not now," he said, looking over her shoulder. "Damn. They've found us."

"Who?" Julie asked an instant before she turned and saw a small media army closing in on them. She reacted instinctively, grabbing the hand Erik held out to her and following him inside the hospital entrance. They made a quick getaway while security detained the press.

"Word has gotten out," Erik said softly as they got on the elevator. It had indeed. Julie noticed the other people in the elevator giving them curious glances as they rode up. This was certainly not the time to discuss their plan of deception with her partner in crime.

They exited at the king's floor. Erik was still preoccupied with the attack of the media. "They'll be after us constantly now, looking for dirt," he said grimly as they walked down the hall. "We'll have to fine tune our strategy."

"That's what I wanted to talk to you about," Julie began. But just then, Erik opened a door, and they were in King Ivar's room.

Erik took one look at his father and felt a rush of relief. The king was out of bed, sitting in a chair by the window. Compared to how he had looked when Erik had last seen him, he was hale and hearty. His color was back, and beneath his beard he was smiling.

Julie's reaction was the opposite of relief. As she set eyes on the king for the first time since his surgery, she thought worriedly that Erik's fears for his father's health had been well-founded. The dignified ruler looked like he'd been on the losing end of a battle. He didn't even get out of his chair when she came into the room, a gesture of chivalry he had never before omitted—which could only mean that he didn't have the strength to do it. He had lost weight, too, and seemed pale. But at least he was smiling.

She smiled back at him, doubly determined to do her part to ensure his recovery.

The king spoke to them both. "If we lived in the bygone days of the arranged marriage, and it had fallen to me to choose a bride for my son, I could not have made a better choice," he said. "Come here, Julie, and give an old man a hug."

Julie was heartened by the strength of his embrace.

Erik watched them, feeling an odd clash of emotions. Their regard for each other was perfectly obvious and perfectly natural. His happiness at his father's approval of Julie was tempered by guiltiness at the deception he had engineered and by worry about how the king would react to their inevitable break up.

He and Julie sat on the sofa, opposite the king. Erik was amazed at how her warmth penetrated the atmosphere in the room; there was none of the sickroom awkwardness that had characterized the previous visits he had made, alone or with Whit. It was as if Julie's smile and conversation banished the shadows.

When the king's doctor poked his head through the doorway, ready to give the update on his father's condition that Erik had requested, Julie was sharing details of the ball with the king. Doubting they'd even miss him, Erik left the room.

Julie watched him go, thinking that he had been no help at all so far. He'd barely said a word, while she had been chattering about any irrelevant detail she could think of. It was safer to keep the conversation focused on the ball, which the king would naturally have an interest in, rather than on the engagement, which would interest him even more. The more she talked, the more she hoped it would distract him from whatever was making him lapse into a frown now and then, a frown that looked disturbingly like the ones she had seen on Whit, Drew and Annah—the people who knew her, or Erik, best.

But her efforts failed. After Erik was gone, King Ivar gave her a penetrating look. "My son made fast work of asking you to marry him. How did all this happen?"

Julie gave a nervous laugh. "The usual way."

"You fell in love?"

"What else?" Julie shifted her position on the sofa. Where was Erik? The king hadn't been asking questions like these when he was around.

The king fell silent for a few moments, then mused, "How well I remember falling in love with my own dear Alexandra, at the Anders Point castle. How I miss her."

Julie leaned over and gave his hand a squeeze.

He patted her hand, then resumed his dignified pose. "It's not hard to imagine any man falling madly in love with you, my dear," the king said, adding bluntly, "But my son doesn't look it."

Julie forced another laugh. "Television," she offered, waving her hand in dismissal. "You can't trust it to give an accurate portrayal. I hear it even puts on ten pounds—"

"On *television* it looked fine," the king interrupted. Then, to Julie's relief, he changed the subject.

Julie's heart was in her throat. Like the others, the king had his suspicions. Like the others, he had seen something that she had missed. What was it?

What it came to Julie when she thought about what the king had seen on television, those brief moments she and Erik had been illuminated on stage at the ball. They had exchanged looks, had touched, had kissed; in short, they had acted like lovers.

Now that she knew what was wrong, what they had to do was plain, as well, if they wanted to be convincing as an engaged couple. And she would have to take charge and do it, knowing full well, from the way he had ended that kiss at the ball, that Erik was not going to like it. Not one bit.

But that was too bad. Time was running out, and with the king right there, there would be no opportunity for a private discussion.

Erik returned to the room and resumed his seat on the couch. With resolve, Julie slid over closer to him. He gave her a questioning glance, then addressed the king. Julie slid closer, until her leg was touching his.

The king had regained his high spirits. "Your gain is my loss," he said to Erik, jokingly. "I'm going to have to find a new caretaker for the Anders Point castle."

Julie joined in his bantering. "Erik said to think of it as a promotion. Didn't you?" she said, smiling at him. Before he realized what was happening, she gave him a soft kiss on the cheek, then linked her hand casually in his.

Erik suddenly became very conscious of the pounding of his blood through his body. Julie's fingers rested lightly in his hand. He was about to pull it away, when he noticed his father looking at their linked hands.

Erik tried to concentrate on the conversation. His father was asking Julie about the news on Anders Point now, and she was filling him in on the details. When Erik shifted restlessly, her fingers began a soothing stroking of his hand.

At least, it must have looked soothing, Erik thought. What it felt like was anything but. The random tracing of her fingertips was slowly driving him mad. Since when could such a tiny caress have such a pronounced effect on him?

He was released from his torment when the king asked to see Julie's ring. But as she held out her hand, Erik found he was powerless to look anywhere but at the curve of her derriere on the sofa next to him as she leaned forward.

"Was it, Erik?" the king asked.

Erik schooled his thoughts. "Was it what, Your Majesty?"

"The ring. Was it from the Constellation Isles?"

"Yes."

"Ah, yes. You can always tell by the craftsmanship." He held Julie's hand in his, turning it gently so that the blue sapphire caught the light. "I assume that it's not by chance that this stone is the color of Julie's eyes."

Julie looked away. Of course it had been chance. Erik had gotten this ring for Roberta. She was nothing but a convenient, and temporary, substitute fiancée.

To her surprise Erik said, "I was very specific about what I wanted for Julie."

Prince Lucas's people had been very accommodating to send him a different ring on such short notice. He had chosen the gem and style he thought would most suit her. His reason, of course, was totally logical. Since she had been reluctant to name her own reward for posing as his fiancée, he planned to let her keep the ring when the engagement ended. He was pleased to find out that she approved of his choice.

Wondering at his answer, Julie sat back again, making sure to settle in at Erik's side. He had his arm across the back of the couch behind her, which looked good. If he would only drop it down across her shoulders, it would look even better. But he hadn't yet made the realization that she had, and he had no other reason to want to put his arm around her, Julie knew. While he discussed the business of the kingdom with his father, she nestled against him, hoping he would take the hint. He didn't, but at least he was chivalrous enough not to pull away from her advances. And the king didn't seem to eye anything askance. In fact, she thought she detected approval in his expression.

After a while a nurse came into the room. "It's time for your walk, Your Majesty. If you prefer, I can come back after your guests leave," she said.

"No, no, not at all," the king said. With her help, he got slowly to his feet.

Erik shot up to his feet at the same time. "How about if I walk with you?" he asked his father. Apparently he would welcome any escape from Julie's caresses—if he even noticed them.

The king shook his head. "I'll just take a spin around the halls with my friend here. Won't be long. You two make yourselves comfortable."

Julie realized that this would be the perfect opportunity to have a private discussion with Erik.

But she didn't get a chance to start it. As soon as King Ivar and the nurse had disappeared into the hallway, Erik yanked her to her feet unceremoniously and pulled her through a nearby doorway. It was the king's closet, she realized just before he closed the door behind them, shrouding them in privacy—and utter darkness. He dropped her hand and asked icily, "Would you mind explaining to me what that was all about?"

At hearing the tension behind his words, she instinctively took a step away from him while she answered. "I was trying to—" she began, but just then she stepped on something soft and squishy, like some kind of animal. Before reason could tell her it was probably the king's slipper, instinct propelled her forward. In an instant, without meaning to, she had fallen into Erik's arms.

He caught her easily, and if he was surprised at the impact, he wasn't thrown off balance by it. Mortified, Julie placed her palms against his chest to steady herself before he would push her away from him.

But he didn't. To her great surprise, he wrapped his arms around her and pulled her tighter against him. She started to speak when she felt his lips come down on hers.

At first her pride asserted itself and she tried to push him away, but the feel of his mouth moving over hers was too powerful a distraction to resist. He was in command, and she followed his lead, responding to the warm, insistent pressure of his lips—tentatively at first, because of how the kiss at the ball had ended. But when his tongue probed at the seam of her lips, she threw caution to the wind and gave him the access he wanted.

This time he didn't pull back. Taking a bold plunge into her mouth, his tongue carried out a seductive strategy, testing her with an advance, tantalizing with a retreat. At the same time his hands roamed over her back, kneading and stroking and coaxing her to surrender more fully to his embrace. Her hands crept up around his neck, and she felt him lean back against the wall as he pulled her even closer.

If he had thought her touches on the couch a tease, he was going through sweet torment right now. He couldn't get enough of the feel of the smooth warmth of her lips, the velvety softness of her tongue. And the friction from the tips of her fingernails grazing over the back of his neck was slowly driving him to distraction. He felt a familiar sensation of gathering need building to a feverish pitch, but never before had it happened to him so quickly, or so intensely. She had bewitched him. He didn't know why; nor did he, at that moment, care to find out.

Suddenly the door to the closet opened. Blinking against the unexpected brightness, Julie saw the king's face. His startled expression quickly gave way to a knowing grin.

"Stay where you are," he said with a chuckle. "I'll just be on my way."

As he closed the door again, Julie heard the nurse say, "Didn't you find your sweater, Your Majesty?"

"Don't need it," the king replied, still chuckling. "Found something that warmed my heart." His voice faded as he left the room again.

Julie relaxed, still leaning against Erik. "We did it," she breathed.

"Not quite," Erik pointed out dryly. "But we were pretty close before the king walked in on us."

Julie felt a flush of embarrassment replace the flush his kiss had brought to her cheeks. She stiffened her arms and pushed herself away from him, then opened up the door again, so that light could filter in. It was maddening to find out that after all those years, one thing hadn't changed—physically, she still found Erik impossible to resist. But he didn't have to know that.

"Being in the closet wasn't my idea, but it fit in nicely with my plan," she said matter-of-factly. "The point is, it worked."

"Your plan?"

"Well, of course. That's why I was...out there on

the couch...I was trying to..." A new flare of embarrassment stopped her.

"Please, go on. Just what exactly *were* you trying to do?"

"My job, Your Highness," she answered coolly. "Didn't you notice the suspicious looks we were getting from my friends and your brother and the king, too, at first? Didn't you wonder what was wrong?"

He had noticed, but had dismissed it as unimportant. If he said he *was* engaged, he expected people to believe he *was* engaged. "What *was* wrong?" he asked cautiously.

"We weren't touching and kissing and—acting like an engaged couple."

He had never thought of that. It made some sense, but still, he resisted. "Roberta and I would never have been all over each other like that," he said in protest.

"You were engaged to Roberta for reasons unknown to me. But you and I are supposed to be engaged because we're in *love*. When we weren't all over each other, people weren't buying it. I finally realized it when you were out of the room, from something the king said."

Erik thought it over. What did he know about being in love? But he knew that his father had seemed more relaxed and jovial during the second part of the visit, when he must have noticed Julie's attentions. And he had been actually delighted when he had walked in on them, just now. Erik had to admit that Julie was on to something.

"I'm afraid I misinterpreted your...actions," he said.

"I'm sorry. It must have seemed like I was throwing myself at you. I tried to tell you what was going on, but I didn't have a chance with the king there," she explained. "And then I stepped on something in the closet, and..." Her voice trailed off.

Erik felt a pang of misgiving. She was not the one who should be apologizing. What had she said? That she was doing him a favor by pretending to be his fiancée. In initiating a display of affection to make sure the king didn't suspect the truth, she had gone above and beyond the call of duty.

And in return, he had nearly gone beyond the bounds of decency. She had only been putting on an act, but there was still no denying the fact that Julie Britton was one powerful temptation. Just as she had when she was sixteen, she had slipped past his guard and taken him to the raw edge of his usually formidable self-control. Well, it was time to put his guard back up, but good. And not just for his own sake.

He reminded himself that this sophisticated woman of the world was really a romantic, small-town girl at heart. After all, she plainly hadn't liked the kiss he had given her after the announcement, and she was fairly glowing with embarrassment after this one. His conscience gnawed at him.

"As for what happened in the closet," he began.

"Just a kiss," she said, dismissing it with a shrug. "Let's not make it into an international incident, Your Highness."

His ego took great exception to her willingness to dismiss so lightly a kiss that he had found nothing short of mind-blowing, but he suspected she did it to save herself any further embarrassment. "If I had foreseen the necessity of public displays of affection, I never would have asked you to—"

Rallying pride made Julie interrupt. "But you did,

and I said yes. Look, Erik, neither one of us *wants* to be in this situation," she said. Summoning the power to resist him physically was one daunting task. "But the way I see it, we have no choice but to make the best of it, for the sake of—"

A noise from the hallway stopped her. It was the king, returning from his walk. Quickly Erik stepped out of the closet, and Julie followed him, trying to straighten her hair.

Once again the king chuckled as he looked at them. When she realized that Erik was about to speak, Julie took his hand and gave it a squeeze to stop him.

"I can't tell you how glad I am that you two came to visit me. I haven't felt this good in longer than I can remember," the king said, beaming his hearty approval.

Erik felt Julie give his hand another squeeze. He looked down at her. She glanced meaningfully at the king, then smiled at Erik, her sparkling blue eyes sending him the message that *this* was what was important. He knew she was right. Nothing else mattered compared to having his father recover his health.

It was with a sense of relief that he looked back at King Ivar. "Sire, may I ask when I may resume my former duties on Isle Anders?" he asked, trying not to sound as eager as he felt.

The king stroked his beard consideringly. "That is just like you, my son. So devoted to duty," he said. "I must admit that I had originally thought of letting you cool your heels in Maine for about a week before sending you home. But your engagement has changed all that."

Erik breathed a sigh of relief. Now that his father approved of the direction he had taken in his personal life, he would get to leave sooner; which not only meant he could resume his old duties, but he could be free of this awkward entanglement with Julie Britton. A long-distance engagement would be preferable by far. "I'm sure I can be in Isle Anders by tomorrow morning."

The king gave another chuckle. "You mistake me, my son. I'm extending your time off, so that you and your fiancée can spend some time alone with each other at the Anders Point castle."

Erik bit back his disappointment. "That's very generous of you, sire, but it isn't necessary."

"I think it is. I don't want anything to distract the two of you from working on your wedding plans."

"But—"

"Because if you don't get a move on...well, let's just say that I don't want the heir to our throne to be sired in a closet."

Erik felt his jaw drop, and a glance next to him showed him that Julie's cheeks were glowing pink. Now he squeezed *her* hand, which had gone limp in his. But before either of them could say anything, the king went on.

"I will visit you there after I am discharged, before my return to Isle Anders." There was dignity in his voice, but an unmistakable twinkle in his eye, as he added, "Go, with my blessing."

After they left, the king's head chef stepped into the room from where he had been waiting in the hall, outside the open door.

King Ivar greeted him, ushering him over to a chessboard in one corner of the room.

"I see you had visitors, Your Majesty," Gustave said, settling into a seat opposite him.

"Tell me, my friend. What do you think of the prince and his lovely lady?" the king asked, stroking his beard thoughtfully.

"They are a perfectly charming couple, Your Majesty. But I must admit there is one thing that bothers me," Gustave said, frowning.

"You are referring, of course, to the fact that they are not really engaged."

"I see your recent illness has not dulled your powers of perception, which does not bode well for my chances in this match," Gustave observed. "I should have known that they would not be able to fool you, Your Majesty."

"No," the king said, in evident satisfaction. "Though they are fooling the rest of the world. Themselves most of all."

"I hope you will be lenient with them. I believe their motive to be most admirable." Gustave showed more tact in his speech than in moving his chess piece. On the next move, the king captured one of his rooks.

"I am aware of that. That is why I am giving them time," the king said.

"You have not yet made them aware of your discovery?"

"That is correct. They have chosen this course. They have discoveries of their own to make."

With that, both men turned their attention to the figures on the board before them.

Chapter Five

Julie hung up the phone and sank down into a kitchen chair, exhausted.

Since she and Erik had flown home from the hospital the day before, the phone in the castle hadn't stopped ringing. A few were follow-up calls from the vendors who had been contracted to work on the ball, but most were friends of Julie calling to congratulate her and wish her well.

She must be turning into a hardened criminal, she mused. Pretending to be Erik's fiancée was becoming second nature, surprisingly. The toughest conversation had been with her parents, who'd heard about the engagement while away on a cruise, the first vacation they had taken in some years. After they got over their initial shock, they were so excited that they wanted to cut their travel short. But Julie wasn't about to let them do that, knowing how long they had been planning and saving for the trip. She managed to talk them into finishing it, without having to resort to confessing that they weren't really going to have Prince Erik for a son-in-law. She felt guilty about the deception, but knew that when the engagement was over, and she could confide in them the whole story, they would understand. Being originally from Anders Point, they both knew and were fond of the king.

Overall, Julie marveled at how smoothly things were going. Since she and Erik had emerged from the closet yesterday, their partnership had been cemented. The reassuring squeeze of his hand when she had needed it had sealed it for her. Like it or not, they were in this thing up to their necks, and at last it really felt as if they were working together. Working for the king—and, in some ways, against the king. Against his finding out the truth, anyway. His well-being was their common, worthy goal.

With relief she realized that Erik was nothing more to her than her fellow conspirator. The kiss she refused to think about. There was no use dwelling on something that had been an isolated incident, an embarrassing misunderstanding no doubt fueled by hormonal overload. He obviously considered it over and done with, and Julie reassured herself that it meant as little to her as it did to him. She was sure that her heart was in no danger, because there was no reason to get her hopes up again. No, she would simply concentrate on doing the job she had agreed to do, and then she and Erik would go their separate ways.

Erik came into the kitchen and gestured toward the phone. "Can't we take that thing off the hook?"

"I'd love to, but what if your father's doctor needs to reach you?"

"You're right, of course. I've just never heard a phone ring so much."

She grinned knowingly. "That's because you never had a sister."

"How many friends do you have, anyway?"

Julie rested her chin on her hands. "Too many that have made the same joke about my finally finding my prince."

"Is that what you've been doing?" he asked with some interest. "Waiting for your prince?"

She dodged that one, which came a little too close for comfort. "That's what all you princes think," she said, going along with the joke. He was beginning to loosen up around her, and she liked that. "That we peasant maidens are just waiting around for you to ride up on your white horses and carry us off to your castles."

"You *are* in my castle," he pointed out.

"Your father's castle," she amended. "And I live here, remember, Your Highness?" she said teasingly.

"The phone stays on the hook."

He held up his hands in mock surrender. "I will say this. Your conversations sound very convincing from this end."

"Thank you, Your Highness. I only live to serve you."

He bowed, grinning. "It is I who am at your service, miss."

Julie decided to take him up on that. "In that case, take a seat so we can have a nice chat."

"And if I refuse your most gracious request?"

"You can't," she said simply. "You've turned my life upside down with this crazy scheme of yours, and you've made me promise to keep it a secret. You're the only one I can talk to about it. If you won't listen to me, Erik, I'm going to explode."

"Well, we can't have that, can we," he said, pulling up a chair. "What do you want to talk about?"

"First of all, the visit to the hospital. How did you think it went with your father?"

"Fine."

"How did you think he looked?"

"Fine."

She looked at him. "Is this going to be one of those conversations where I talk and you grunt out one-syllable answers?"

"Are there other kinds?"

She sighed. "Not with men."

"Okay. Let me ask a question. How did *you* think it went with my father?"

"He really seemed tickled by the whole thing." Especially about finding them in the closet, she thought. "I'm not sure he'll be so happy when it ends, though," she said with a worried look. "Which reminds me. Erik, how long are you planning on having this last?"

"Just until the king is well enough to resume ruling, which may not be too far away, from the report his doctor gave me yesterday. I'll wait a decent interval before breaking it off, of course. But we won't have to live together here after he goes home to Isle Anders. I'm sure that by then he'll change his mind about having me resume my former duties and ask me to go back with him."

Julie wished that what he said was true, but she wasn't counting on it. "What about what he said about wanting us to make wedding plans?"

Erik dismissed her worry. "We can stall him on that," he said confidently. "He knows there is no real reason for me to get married in a hurry. I don't have to be married until I assume the throne, and now that he is making such a fine recovery, that will probably be years from now.''

He looked so pleased about that, that Julie thought this might be a good time to bring something up. ''Not all of the phone calls have been for me, you know,'' she said. ''One came for you while you were running this morning.''

''Who was it? Another one of my friends joking about my finally finding my peasant maiden?''

''Very funny. Actually, it was Roberta.''

His expression turned sour. ''What did *she* want?''

''She heard the news and wanted to congratulate you.''

''She's got a lot of nerve calling here, after what she did,'' he growled.

''Don't be too hard on her, Erik. She's in love. And she still wants to be friends with you.''

''Yeah? Well, in my book, *friends* don't go back on their word and leave you twisting in the wind.''

''She feels bad about that. She's glad things turned out for you.''

Erik looked at her through narrowed eyes. ''Sounds like the two of you had a real cozy chat.'' He wasn't sure he liked the idea of his almost fiancée and his pretend fiancée getting so chummy. ''Did you tell her the real story?''

''Of course not,'' Julie said, indignant. ''I told her what I've told everyone—that we've known each other for years, but never realized until the ball that we had a future together, which as you know is perfectly true.'' Of course, the ''future'' they'd found together wasn't quite what it appeared to the world. After a moment Julie said, ''Roberta hoped you would understand that she never meant to hurt you.''

"You know what's hard to understand?" Erik said impatiently. "I think she knew all along that I would treat her better than that jerk she's been pining over all these years. But she still dumped me for him. Go figure."

"It's not to understand or not understand," Julie tried to explain. Erik thought everything could be reduced to logic, while she knew, from experience, that love defied it. "It just *is*. When you're in love, all the king's horses and all the king's men couldn't keep you from your destiny."

He said nothing, but then, he didn't have to. From the look on his face, it was completely obvious what he thought about *love*.

"That doesn't justify what she did to you," Julie was quick to add. "She had no right to make you a promise that she couldn't keep."

"Damn straight. But at least it showed me I was wrong about her. She was not at all the kind of woman I need as a partner."

"Don't you mean 'wife'?"

"For a prince, a wife is a partner," he said. "Getting married is my duty, and what I need most is a woman who will fulfill hers."

Julie rolled her eyes. This ought to be good, she thought. "Describe for me this ideal 'partner' of yours."

Erik propped his foot up on one of the chairs. "Why?"

She improvised. "So I can do a good job impersonating her."

"You're doing fine."

"Humor me."

He began with reluctance. "Well, the most important

thing for me is that I be able to trust her—to honor her word and to do her duty.''

''Being a charming hostess, making babies, looking adoringly at you—''

''Look, being a prince makes me an anachronism, but I'm not a Neanderthal. I don't want a woman hovering over me. Providing heirs to the throne is a duty of mine, so of course my wife would have to want children. That would have to be agreed before the marriage. Other than that, I would expect her to have her own life, her own interests, her own civic or charitable responsibilities, even her own career, if she so chooses.''

Sounded reasonable so far, Julie thought.

Erik went on. ''Of course, she would be representing me and Isle Anders in the public eye, so it's very important that she possess a certain amount of poise.''

''Naturally. You wouldn't want someone slurping her soup at all those state dinners,'' Julie said with a grin. ''What else?''

''That's it.''

''Aren't you forgetting something?''

He looked at her blankly.

''What about your feelings for each other?''

''I think all of the above assumes a mutual respect and loyalty.''

''Nothing more?''

''Like what?'' he said, so irritably that she knew he knew darn well what she was getting at.

''What else? Love!''

''That's got nothing to do with it.''

''It has *everything* to do with it.''

He shook his head. ''Not for me. Finding a woman who is suitable will be enough.''

"Your father married for love," she reminded him.

"And look what happened."

"Yes, look. He married and lived happily with the woman he loved for the rest of her life," Julie pointed out. Erik might not want to admit it, but she could read between the lines and see that the real reason for his views on marriage had nothing whatever to do with duty. His father's pain at the loss of the love of his life must have been immense, and Erik had no doubt shared that pain. That would explain a lot. Marriage itself was risky enough; no wonder love would be out of the question for him. Loving someone would leave him too vulnerable to losing and being hurt. Duty was safer.

"That's not what I meant. My mother was a wonderful person, but she was not a good choice for a queen. She tried her best to do as she was expected, but the whole world knew her to be...unconventional."

"She endeared herself to the world, because she wasn't all proper and stuffy." What he said was undeniable, but Julie sprang to his mother's defense because she had always admired her. "I'm sure your father never regretted his choice for one moment."

"No. But ever since she died, things have been different in the family. More dignified and staid. I can only wonder if that is the way he really wanted things all along."

Julie doubted it, but saw that there would be no getting through to Erik. She sighed.

"Anyway, it is of no concern," he said with utter finality. "As required, before my coronation I will marry the woman I feel is most suitable. For now, I am very grateful to you for helping me get my father recovered and back on the throne." With that he left.

Julie went to work updating her inventory of the

wine cellar. But she couldn't stop thinking about what Erik had said. There was no arguing that he was a man of duty; but he wasn't one dimensional. The views he had expressed were in direct opposition to the sensitivity that had once drawn her to him. She was sure there was a softer, more emotional side of him, which he had suppressed. She vowed to herself to try, during their time together, to bring that side out. She wanted him to see that deep down he believed in much more than duty. She couldn't believe that he would be truly happy in a duty-only marriage; and even though she knew now that she didn't love him, she still had a high regard for him and wished him happiness. It would give her great satisfaction if, when he someday married someone, he did it for love.

It was a tall order. But it would give her something to do other than mark time until she was no longer his fiancée.

Although she didn't realize it at first, Julie got her first chance a few days later, when she locked herself out of the castle.

"At least having Erik here will save me a walk into town," she grumbled to herself.

She rang the front bell, but got no answer. He was there, she knew. Wondering if the bell was broken, she tried knocking. She was banging on the door with her fist when she heard a voice behind her.

"There's no one in there."

She spun around and saw Erik standing behind her, with a garden rake in one hand. "I thought *you* were in there," she said. "I'm locked out. Would you open the door for me?"

"I would, if I had my keys with me."

"You don't? Why not?"

"I thought *you* were in there," he said. While she was taking a shower, he had decided to tidy up the outside a bit in the wake of a thunderstorm the night before. Because he'd sent the staff away, Erik was tending to the task himself. But he was glad to do it because he was full of restless energy he needed to expend. He was used to having much more to do; and besides, he thought getting outside would dispel his mental image of how Julie looked in the shower.

Now here she was standing in front of him, in jeans and a yellow top that clung in all the right places. The tendrils of hair that always seemed to escape her braid to frame her face were still damp and curling slightly, and her eyebrows were drawn together into an adorable frown. He didn't know how she always managed to look wholesome and sexy at the same time.

"I guess I've locked you out, too," she said. "Sorry. I'm on my way into town to do story time at the library. I'll walk down—I can make it on time if I hurry—and then I'll bring the key back with me when I'm finished." She paused, then added, casually, "Of course, if you don't want to wait, you can walk to town with me and get the key yourself."

"Where?"

"From the sheriff."

"Your friend Drew?"

"Yes," Julie said, starting down the driveway. She looked back over her shoulder. "Are you coming?"

He hesitated. He had finished up his work, so there was nothing more for him to do outside the castle, but he had his reasons for not wanting to go into town with her.

She smiled to herself, watching his inner debate. It

was easier to steer clear of each other when they were alone at the castle. In town, there were lots of people who knew the king. They would have to act like a happily engaged couple. "I can't blame you for being chicken," she teased. "If you go into town you might have to—gasp!—*touch* me," she said, rolling her eyes in mock horror. "Stay here, Erik! Save yourself from such a horrible fate!"

"I'm not chicken," he insisted, chagrined that she had hit on the reason for his reluctance—yet had misunderstood it. It wasn't that he didn't *want* to touch her—it was that he was afraid that once he started, he wouldn't want to stop. "I've got dirt all over my hands," he said, holding them up.

"You are a mess," she agreed laughingly. "No one will believe you are really a prince, looking like that. But if you hurry, I'll wait while you wash up at the outside faucet."

He ended up coming with her, and Julie smiled to herself as they walked along the road to town. Getting him into Anders Point was a great idea. After all, it was his mother's hometown, so there would be lots to remind him of her. And folks who remembered her loved to tell stories about her. All that would chip away at his heart of stone.

So would the kids at her story time, not that she thought she could get him there. She was trying to think of a plan when he spoke.

"What is story time all about?"

"I read to a group of preschoolers once a week at the library."

"Is that part of your job?"

"No. I'm a reading teacher during the school year, but this is something I volunteered to do for the summer. Anything you do to get kids interested in books early on helps them later. Something I'm sure you are aware of, with the high literacy rate you have on Isle Anders."

They had come to Drew's house, the first one on the outskirts of the town. Anyone could be watching them now. He looked at her. "May I take your hand?" he asked formally.

"If we're engaged, you don't have to ask," she reminded him, placing her hand in his.

He made no comment, but after a minute went back to the previous topic. "Do you like teaching?"

"I love it. If I hadn't been able to keep working in education, I wouldn't have accepted your father's offer of the caretaking job at the castle."

"Then he talked you into planning the ball."

"Getting to do that was the chance of a lifetime."

"And here I thought you were going to be an actress," he said, giving her hand a squeeze.

Julie knew that the warmth in her cheeks was from more than just the sunshine. It was the first time he had referred to the night of that other, long-ago ball, albeit indirectly. She had told him that, and more, while they were dancing. She couldn't believe he remembered it, after all this time. "Oh, I outgrew that dream, along with a few others," she said, with a little laugh at herself. "Story time is about as close to acting as I get." Except for the role of his fiancée, she thought.

"Maybe I'll come and watch," he said, grinning.

That, of course, was exactly what she was hoping. But she casually pooh-poohed the idea. "You'd better not. You wouldn't like it."

He wasn't used to being told what to do, and obviously didn't like it. "How do you know?"

She shrugged. "It's just me and a bunch of kids," she said. "I know how you feel about me, and I assume you have no interest in children—other than your own, of course."

He frowned. "Why do you say that?"

"Because your children will be the heirs to the throne. As you said, they'll be your *duty*." She spoke as casually as she could, while wondering whether he would rise to the bait. "These are just ordinary kids."

He frowned. She made it sound like he was a machine. "Providing heirs *is* my duty, but I happen to like kids," he said, a little defensively.

She pretended not to hear. They were in front of the town hall now. "Do you know where the sheriff's office is?" she asked. "First floor, second door. If Drew isn't in there, just ask anyone where she is."

"Anyone?"

"This is a small town. Ask a few anyones, and someone will be able to tell you," she said, smiling. "I'll see you when I get back to the castle." Or sooner, she hoped.

"Wait a minute," he said.

She turned back, and he took both of her hands. "The two white-haired ladies sitting on the porch across the street have their eyes glued on us," he murmured. "I think I had better kiss you."

She tried not to laugh, but didn't succeed. "Sounds like an engagement emergency to me," she said. "Kiss away."

But she wasn't laughing a minute later, when he released her and walked away. Damn, but the man had talent. She had to uncurl her toes so that she could walk down the street to the library.

Later he showed up at story time, as she had hoped.

He came into the room just as she was about to begin the last story. He leaned over and whispered to her, "I thought it would look bad if I didn't stay to walk you back."

"How flattering," she whispered back.

He sat down in the back, trying to be inconspicuous, but the ten children sitting in a circle on the floor would not have it. They all turned around to stare at him, then started to speak.

"Who are you?" one little girl asked.

"He's the prince, silly," another told her.

"How come your mother or father didn't bring you?" another one wanted to know.

"You need a name tag," one boy informed him. "Miss Julie helped all of us make name tags. See?"

At last, Julie got them settled down, and soon they were all engrossed in the story. Some of them stretched out on the rug, and one little boy wandered back to where Erik was sitting and wormed his way onto his lap. He leaned back against Erik and listened, enthralled, busily sucking on the thumb that he had popped into his mouth. Julie silently blessed the little guy, after seeing the look that passed across Erik's face. He schooled it back into careful control, of course, but for a moment there he couldn't have looked more pleased if he had been awarded the Nobel Prize.

What is happening to me? Erik wondered. He was used to being a busy man of affairs, brusque and efficient, involved in issues of international magnitude, weighing important decisions. He liked that. But here he was, in a tiny town in Maine that escaped the notice of the world, sitting on the floor in a stuffy back room in a run-down library with a lapful of sweaty little boy snuggled against him, listening to a story about a lost pig. It was amazing, when he thought about it. And the amazing part was that he liked it.

Julie was pretty amazing, too. She was really into the story, her animated expressions and versatile voice a miracle cure for even the toughest case of the won't-sit-stills. The kids were spellbound, and he had to admit that he was close to it himself. Not so much that he wanted to hear how the story turned out, although he did, but more because Julie had bound him in her spell.

She had seemed different the night of the ball, less than one week ago—sophisticated and cool, efficient and a little standoffish. He would never have involved her in his scheme if he had realized then that she was still as warmhearted and unpretentious, unabashedly honest and thoroughly likable as he remembered. Just by being herself, she could easily lure him into feeling too much, and that's what made it so dangerous to be around her. But he was on guard against that; all her appeal could not sway him from his duty. Once more she had captured his interest, but that was all. She was far from the kind of woman he eventually would marry.

But he had to admit that despite that fact, this engagement was working somehow. Funny, how that was.

From that day, Erik went into town regularly, both with Julie and on his own. On more than one occasion, she knew, some of the old-timers had been bending his ear about his mother, his father and things that had happened during earlier times. And he always seemed to find some excuse or other to show up for at least part of story time each week. Together they had attended town meetings, the July Fourth parade and the blueberry festival. He had even come to the church rummage sale where Julie was working as a volunteer.

After the initial flurry of interest, the town had accepted them. No rumors of the truth about their engagement would reach the king from that quarter.

Out in public as often as they were, touching each other had become part of their daily lives. Still, an unexpected caress from Erik, or the brush of his lips against her cheek, never failed to make Julie's heart trip along faster. Reaching out to hold his hand and then having him put his arm around her, anchoring her to his side, made her feel things that a pretend fiancée was foolish to feel. She might have felt cherished, but she was, at most, appreciated. Not that that was all bad. Although he remained restrained, at least Erik didn't shrink from touching her. He liked her, she could tell. And she was pleased to see the progress she was making in softening him up.

Walking back to the castle after the annual Anders Point Lobsterfest, he was in an especially good mood. He had been talking fishing all night, a subject that interested him not only because it was one of the major industries on Isle Anders, but also because it was a hobby of his.

"Lester Cranston is going to take me out on his boat tomorrow," he said. "I'll be leaving early, so I'll try not to wake you up."

"I'm used to your getting up early by now," she said. "And the sun usually wakes me, anyway."

"I'm not surprised, with all the windows there are in that room. Why don't you order curtains?"

She looked at him. "When you lived in the tower room, did you want curtains?" she said simply.

She had him there. "No," he admitted. "But if you—"

"I don't. Remember, I lived in the city most of my life. I'll wake up with the sun every day for the rest of it, if I can wake up to a view like this." She spread her hand out, encompassing the ocean that spread out below them. When she stumbled over a rock in the gravel road, he took her hand to steady her.

"Careful, there," came his voice from beside her, soft and low. To her surprise he didn't let go, but kept her hand in his. Not since the time in the hospital closet had he touched her when they weren't in public.

He didn't know why he kept ahold of her hand, except that it felt right. They walked along in the darkness, with the ever present sound of the ocean as background noise. They were past all the houses now, so they might have been the only two people in the world. To dispel the growing intensity of the moment, he turned to her and said, "By the way, nice shirt."

"Thanks," she said with an impish grin. She had worn the shirt on purpose and had been wondering when he would notice it.

"It looks familiar," he said dryly. It was, in fact, one of his T-shirts. It was huge on her, but it still looked good. Maybe a little too good. "Are you going to make a habit of swiping things from my drawers?"

"An engaged man should expect his fiancée to lay claim to his wardrobe," she said archly. "It's one of the rights and privileges that goes with the territory."

"I must have missed that clause in the rule book."

"Don't be stingy."

"I'm not stingy. It's my favorite T-shirt, but you can have it if you want, and not just because you made a mess of it eating lobster tonight."

"You miss the point. I don't want to own it—I want to wear it because it's *yours*." She caught herself and added, "I mean, that's how a real fiancée would feel."

He didn't answer, but seemed to be thinking about what she said. "It's funny how things turned out," she went on. "We agreed to a fake engagement, but when you made that announcement, we became engaged in the eyes of the world. And here we are behaving as if we were in love." She paused. "You know, it's a lot easier than I thought it would be."

As if by accord, they had stopped walking. She looked up at him, trying to read his sober expression. "What about you?" she prompted. She wanted him to admit, at least to himself, that tenderness of feeling wasn't totally alien to him. She wanted him to realize that if he could *act* like he was in love, he could fall in love for real someday.

Erik looked down at her sweet smile, hating himself at that moment for ever getting her involved in this. She was right; it was easy. Too easy, and that was the problem. The woman he had pictured for his pretend fiancée would have found enforced public affection awkward and distasteful. But for warmhearted Julie, it was easy. It was easy for him, too, but for a different reason. Any contact with her, however innocent, helped him slake to some degree his mounting lust for her. He liked having an excuse to touch her, because he found her so damned touchable.

Her words contained a warning too explicit not to heed. He dropped her hand and said matter-of-factly, "It's easy *because* it's not real. There are none of the uncertainties or risks that go along with real love. You and I both know exactly how this engagement is going to end."

It was a reminder as chilling as a slap from a cold wave in the ocean. After that, Julie wrapped her arms around herself and walked back to the castle, by Erik's side, but not connected to him by word or touch.

Chapter Six

There was a surprise waiting for them back at the castle; lying at the bottom of the stone steps that led to the front door, panting, was a dog.

His coat was matted and tangled, as if it had been wet and dried several times. When the dog saw them, he got up and began wagging his tail tentatively, hopefully.

"Oh, the poor thing." Julie murmured, squatting down and holding out her hand.

But he didn't even seem to notice her. Instead, he slunk over to stand in front of Erik.

Erik looked down at the dog. "Hello, boy," he said. "Time for you to go home now." He pointed down the drive. "Go on home."

The dog didn't move. He just looked up beseechingly at Erik, belly on the ground in the classic dog pose of humble servility.

Julie watched, fascinated. Just when she had been ready to give up on Erik's ever feeling anything more than duty, here came a situation that would tug on anyone's heartstrings. She curbed the impulse to take over and help the dog, waiting to see how Erik answered the creature's silent plea.

The dog didn't budge. "He won't go home," Erik said to Julie.

"Maybe he's lost. I've never seen him around here before," she offered. "Look, there's a rabies-shot tag on his collar, but no license and no identification."

"What do you think we should do?"

Julie didn't say a word, just looked at him.

He held up his hands as if warding off her thoughts. "Oh, no," he said. "We're not taking him into the castle."

"We're not?"

"No way."

"Your mother—" she began.

He interrupted her. "My softhearted mother made an international spectacle of the family the time the animal shelter on Isle Anders was flooded out, and she brought all the animals into the castle to live with us." His father, naturally, had indulged her.

"It was wonderful."

Erik might have known Julie would think that. She would no doubt do the same thing herself. "It was chaos," he said in contradiction, although he remembered that to him and Whit it had been chaos of the most wonderful kind. "My father had to put official business on hold for weeks."

"But this is only one dog. And he doesn't seem prone to causing chaos."

The dog was, in fact, licking Erik's shoelaces. "Hey, stop that," Erik told him, moving away. The dog moved over to position himself in front of him again.

"Looks like he's bowing to you, Your Highness," Julie said with a grin.

"He's a damned nuisance."

"Then you'd better get rid of him," Julie said decidedly, trying a new tactic. "You're absolutely right. Since he won't leave on his own, the only alternative is to call the sheriff. Drew will drop him off at the animal shelter."

"What's it like?"

She shrugged. "About what you would expect."

"Are they going to put him in a cage?"

"It's not a five-star hotel, Erik. But they treat the animals well. If they can't find his owner, they'll try to find him a good home." She paused, then added, "I'm sure you're right. He can't stay here."

Then she stretched and forced herself to yawn. "All of a sudden, I'm awfully tired. If it's all right with you, I think I'll go to bed."

"Go ahead," he said. "I'll take care of this matter." Just like he took care of the "matter" of getting engaged, Julie thought. Duty calls. But at the doorway she glanced back, and saw him bending down to scratch the dog's ears.

When she went downstairs the next morning, the dog was wolfing down cold cereal and milk out of a mixing bowl in the corner of the kitchen floor.

Erik was eating his at the table, with a spoon. "It seemed a little late to call Drew last night," he explained. "I'll take him over to the shelter myself later this morning."

"Good plan," Julie said, smiling to herself. But later that morning the dog had devoured most of the food in the house, grudgingly submitted to the indignity of a bath, chewed on Erik's running shoes and acquired a name—Rufus, which was the sound he made when he barked. It was with no surprise but a great deal of satisfaction that Julie saw Erik come back from the animal shelter with Rufus still in tow.

"I couldn't leave him," he said. "It looked like it would get awfully hot in there by afternoon."

Julie refrained from pointing out that the animal shelter was air-conditioned. "Whatever you think is best," she said amiably.

"The vet that checked him out thought it would be fine. Meanwhile, the folks at the shelter are sending out information on him, and keeping an eye out for any reports of lost dogs that match his description. I imagine it won't be much longer until his family comes to claim him."

But days went by and no one did. Rufus became a hairy, playful, hungry part of their lives. Erik took care of the dog without complaint. And although he frequently alluded to the fact that the arrangement was only temporary, Julie was secretly delighted. When they walked through town, hand in hand, with Rufus dogging his royal master's footsteps, Erik could rationalize all he wanted about how their having a dog made the engagement look all the more real. She knew Rufus was softening up his heart, one lick on the face at a time.

In fact, she'd lay odds that Rufus's stay in Erik's life would be far less temporary than her own.

Julie stopped by for coffee early each morning before Annah opened, while Erik was out running—with Rufus, of course. More often than not, Drew showed up also, and the three of them talked while Lexi prowled around the secondhand shop in search of "princess clothes."

"Annah, I'd like to take a look in back this morning," Julie said one day. "Erik and I are going to a dinner in Boston on Saturday, and I need something to wear."

"Help yourself," Annah said. "I've gotten some new things in since the ball that you might like. Set aside whatever you want. I'll be back later in the morning, after I finish up here."

"You're a doll."

Annah shrugged off her thanks. "What kind of friend would I be, if I didn't do you a favor now and then?"

Julie turned to Drew. "Speaking of favors," she began.

"Me first," Drew interrupted. "Would you watch Lexi for me on Monday? I've got to spend the day in court."

"Absolutely," Julie said. Then she noticed that Lexi was peeking through the doorway from the back, listening. "Prince Erik and I have been hoping Princess Lexi would be able to pay us a visit in the castle," she added. Satisfied, Lexi grinned and disappeared again.

"Great," Drew said. "Now what can I do for you?"

"I was wondering if you would take care of Rufus on Saturday, while Erik and I are in Boston. None of the castle staff are on duty right now and we can't leave him alone."

"Do you mean that the royal hound isn't invited?" Drew asked dryly. "I didn't think the prince made a move without him. Sure, I can watch him for you. Lexi will be thrilled."

"I think Rufus likes her second best," Julie said, smiling. "Thanks, Drew."

Lexi, who had come bouncing back into the front room for a glass of milk, piped up, "I know who Rufus likes first best. The same person you do, Julie."

Remarks like that never failed to remind Julie of the deceptive life she was leading. She sidestepped them with regularity. "Do you think he'll give Rufus a ring, too?" she joked.

Lexi giggled and left the room again. Julie concentrated on her coffee. She wondered what her friends were thinking, really thinking, about her engagement to Erik. Drew seemed to have accepted it. Her busy life as a single mother with a full-time job didn't leave her much time for idle speculation.

But Annah was another matter. Keen insight like hers was worrisome, especially given its focus on matters of the heart. She didn't say much, but from the look on her face sometimes, Julie wondered whether she suspected that the whole thing was a fake. The truth was, she didn't know which would bother her more— that Annah discerned that she really didn't love Erik or that she really did.

"Get up on the wrong side of the bed this morning, Your Highness?" Julie asked, giving Erik a saucy grin from her seat next to him in the jet.

If she was trying to cajole him into a better humor, he wished her good luck. He knew he was in a foul mood, but he had good reason to be. First of all, he hated glad-handing and empty chatter like the one they were going to in Boston. All that glad-handing and empty chatter was Whit's territory. The fact that the king hadn't shown a sign of changing his mind about swapping their duties back again was the second reason Erik was in a funk. Thirdly, he'd had to leave Rufus behind. He knew Drew would take good care of him, and he'd have fun romping with her daughter, but still, he had whined when Erik had left him.

Erik frowned. Those three reasons were irritating as hell, but he knew that they alone, even in combination, weren't the real reason he was under a black cloud. His main problem wasn't that he had gotten up on the wrong side of the bed, it was that he was the only one in his bed. If he had been even half as attracted to another woman as he was to Julie, he would have done something about it long before now. But in this case his hands were tied, as much by her sweet wholesomeness as by the awkward situation they were in. Not to mention the fact that he had no idea whether she felt the same way about him. Since that kiss in the hospital closet, they had shared countless public caresses, but she seemed oblivious to their having any effect, other than to serve to make legitimate the pretend engagement.

It was bad enough living with her at the castle day after day and sharing casual affection in Anders Point's down-home, down-East element. Those who traveled in the exclusive circle that was invited to this dinner, however, would expect restrained formality in an engagement like theirs. But restraint, which was usually second nature to Erik, would be hard-won tonight, especially with Julie in the dress she was wearing. It wasn't outright naughty—more like subtly provocative—but it flirted with the limits of his self-control.

No wonder he prowled around like a caged tiger in his father's room, when they stopped by to see him in Boston. Shortly after their last hospital visit, the king's doctor had moved him to an exclusive convalescent center in the city, and his recovery was proceeding apace. His father, jovial as he had been the last time they'd seen him, made another vague reference to visiting them at the castle in Maine before he went home to Isle Anders, which did not improve Erik's mood. He and Julie were sleeping in adjoining bedrooms in case of that visit or one by Whit, though Erik thought neither situation was really likely to happen. And naturally, living in such close quarters with Julie only intensified his problem.

At the end of the visit, the king suggested that they forego taking the limo and walk to the dinner instead. "It's just across the way," he said, pointing out the window.

Erik wasn't sure it was such a good plan, but didn't want to cross his father. The king's progress was good, but until he had been given a clean bill of health, Erik didn't want to do anything that might rock the boat.

Julie had mentioned on the way in that she had never seen the Public Garden, so he knew how she would answer before he turned to her and asked, "What would you say to a little sight-seeing?"

It was their first public appearance since the ball, other than at remote Anders Point, which wasn't the same thing. It didn't take long for them to be noticed, and before long Erik saw an approaching media cluster. They had dodged the cameras their last time in the city, but he knew they had no hope of escape now. He was used to this kind of attention himself—not that he liked it—but he hated having to put Julie through it.

His worries, it turned out, were completely unfounded. Julie was a natural—as gracious and poised as a princess should be, but smiling, spirited and so *real.* When she stopped in front of a flower bed filled with a profusion of blossoms and smiled beguilingly up at him, he knew that image would grace the front page of newspapers everywhere the next morning. No one heard her whisper, "How am I doing?" right before she planted an impulsive kiss on his cheek. He had given her an encouraging wink, unable to put into words all that was crowding his mind.

Later, when they arrived at the hotel where the dinner was taking place, he said, "You almost had me convinced out there. How do you do it?"

She had raised one eyebrow. "That's how a woman in love with you would act."

He was glad that, with introductions to be made, he didn't have to admit even to himself how good it had felt.

The dinner turned out better than Erik expected because his friend Prince Lucas, whom he hadn't seen for some time, was there. His brother had also managed to show up by the time the dancing started. He was going to visit the king the next day, Whit explained, and since he had gotten in early he thought he might as well stop by.

Julie gave Erik a secret wink, and he remembered her saying that his brother wasn't one to miss a good party. Then she excused herself to freshen up. In Erik's eyes she didn't need any freshening, although he appreciated her being gone for a while, so that the men in the room would have a chance to notice one of the other women for a change.

The three men stood together, off to one side. Erik noticed that Lucas had been silent and brooding most of the evening, and it wasn't too hard to guess why.

His friend was the ruler of the Constellation Isles, a cluster of islands that together made up a country that was the closest neighbor of Isle Anders. Upon the unexpected death of his father, Prince Lucas had been given provisional rule of the country for one year—by the end of which time he had to marry or else relinquish the throne. Erik probably understood better than anyone how unpalatable Lucas found his position. What was worse, time was running out for his friend, who now had mere months to wed in order to keep his crown. No one likes to have his hand forced—especially not a prince.

"How is the search for a wife going?" Erik asked him.

"Not as well as yours did," Lucas noted, neatly turning the attention away from his situation. "Congratulations, Erik. There's not another woman like her in the room."

Maybe not in the whole world, Erik thought. One thing was for sure—Julie was unique.

"Did you actually meet her at the ball?" Lucas asked.

His friend's question sounded so casual, but Erik thought he understood what was behind it. If Lucas had wanted to be, he could have been married long before now, his crown secure. But he was still searching. Erik shook his head. "She's from Anders Point, so I've known her for years."

"He knew her because she was a friend of mine," Whit said.

"But I decided not to hold that against her," Erik remarked dryly.

Whit grinned and said to Lucas, "I keep telling him he doesn't deserve her."

After a pause, Lucas said, "All the more reason not to take her for granted."

After that, the subject changed to matters of state, but Erik found his mind wandering back to that last comment. Lucas was a good friend, and he had a few years on him, so what he said had an impact. Of course, Lucas didn't know how things really were between him and Julie. Erik could never take for granted how well she was playing her part.

A feminine voice behind him intruded on his thoughts. "...our friend Roberta. Have you heard? After their elopement last month, he's already left her for..."

Erik hadn't known about that. He felt a moment of pity for Roberta, even though he, more than anyone, knew that she had chosen her own course, foolish though it was. Another victim of love.

Growing impatient, Erik scanned the crowd to see if Julie was on her way back yet. She was taking a long time, it seemed to him. He knew Julie; she wasn't one to take forever primping. Finally he saw her coming toward him, but she got stuck in a crowd. After she had stood there a moment, the man next to her started talking to her.

When Erik saw who it was, he left Whit and Lucas without a word and started toward Julie. It was the same philandering duke who had hit on her at the ball. That time, he had exercised restraint. This time, seeing the guy with Julie put the capper on his sour mood. He knew him too well to doubt his motive.

He fought his way through the crowd of cameras that had been following Julie around all evening.

"No, I do not," Julie was saying as she pulled her arm away from the man. Stepping deliberately between her and the duke, Erik draped his arm across her shoulders and pulled her to his side. He spoke to the duke in a voice so low that no one else but Julie could hear it.

"I consider myself to be a fair and patient man, but you have stepped over the line," he said.

The duke gulped, his Adam's apple bobbing up and down. "I didn't mean anything, Your Highness. I swear."

Julie hadn't liked the duke's presumptive touch or his sly suggestion that they go outside to get a breath of fresh air, and had been about to tell him to stuff it when Erik had shown up like an avenging Norse god. She didn't want any trouble, but trouble was likely to erupt if she didn't dampen the powder keg Erik's temper had been riding on all day. She tried to avert his attention from the duke. "Erik, let's—"

He ignored her and addressed the duke again. "If I *weren't* such a fair and patient man, pal, the paparazzi would all be getting a raise tomorrow, when their editors got their photos of my fist connecting with your face," he said, nodding his head toward the crowd of photographers.

Most of the color drained from the duke's face.

"But," Erik continued, "because of my *patience* they will be able to report only that you were seen being escorted from the room by me. Does that seem *fair* to you?"

The duke nodded.

"Don't make a move," Erik warned. "I'll be right back." Then he hustled Julie through the crowd.

Julie, crushed to his side, was relieved that he hadn't resorted to blows. The duke might have outweighed him, but Erik would have pulverized the guy, especially in the mood he was in. "Where are we going?" she asked him.

"To Lucas or Whit, whoever I find first. They're the only ones I trust to watch you while I take care of this—"

"Matter," Julie finished for him. Again, duty called. "I had things under control, not that that matters to you, I realize. I never knew you had such a jealous streak." If she didn't know better, she would be flattered.

"This isn't jealousy. This is possessiveness."

"There's a difference?"

There was a huge difference, as any man knew. "Jealousy is when you want something that belongs to someone else. Possessiveness is when you protect something that belongs to you."

Julie gulped at that thought. Next thing she knew, she was standing with Whit as Erik headed back through the crowd.

"That was a close one," she said, watching him.

"Yeah. I could see the headlines. Prince Dukes It Out With Duke." Whit's grin faded as he shook his head. "You know, I think you're really done it, Julie."

"Done what?" she said. "Started World War III?" Whit's grin reappeared, but only fleetingly. "No," he said soberly. "You've made my brother love you." Julie's denial stuck in her throat. Could Erik really be doing such a good job of acting? So good that he would even fool his own brother?

"What tipped you off?" she asked Whit, keeping her tone light.

Her childhood friend looked down on her with tender regard. "He's very protective of the people he loves," he said.

There *was* only one reason why Whit's words could create a swell of hope in Julie so strong that it made her reel, physically. She had been fighting it, but it had grown stronger with each passing day she spent with Erik. What she had been denying was all too true. She didn't just want to help him be able to fall in love— she wanted him to fall in love with *her*. It wasn't a girlhood fantasy anymore, to become his bride. It was as real as a rainbow, a shooting star, a moonbeam.

She, Julie Briton, had fallen in love with Erik Anders, twice and for all. She was so good at acting like a woman in love because she was no longer acting at all. It felt good to stop resisting and finally admit it to herself. It felt scary, too. Her hope that he might someday be able to fall in love with her was fragile indeed, despite what Whit had said. But where there's love there's hope.

Buoyed by hope, Julie felt like she was floating in Erik's arms after he came back to claim her and led her onto the dance floor. "Thank you for coming to my rescue," she said.

"Aren't you going to tell me that you could have taken care of it yourself?"

Julie smiled. "I could have. But I liked having you take care of me. It was—" She stopped. It had been exhilarating. She was perfectly capable of going through life without Erik, but with him everything was more intense. Her range of feelings opened up to include heights she had never before experienced. She wondered if he might someday feel that way about her.

"It was what?" he prompted.

"It was exactly how a man in love would act."

"Really?" he said, concentrating on the dance. "I wouldn't know."

"Maybe you will someday."

"No, Julie."

"Are you telling me that you don't believe in love at all?" Her words were quiet, but she pressed closer against him, feeling the strength and hardness of his body against hers. And the warmth. It was unexpected, the heat she felt flowing through him. This man might be as solid as a rock, but she just knew he couldn't have a heart of stone.

Gathering her close, he moved one hand up to the back of her neck, and she felt the warmth of his breath against her ear. "I believe in love, Julie," he said in a low voice. "I believe in love of family, love of country, love of children, love of the earth."

At his words she felt another bubbling rush that carried her along, floating, all the while she was held firmly in his arms. "And between a man and a woman?" she whispered.

He cradled her hand in his own bigger one. It was strong as any hand she had ever known, yet the gentle touch of his thumb gave her a new awareness of how sensitive the flesh of her palm was. "I believe in many things between a man and a woman," he said grittily.

Julie closed her eyes, taking silent pleasure in the things he was making her feel. She believed in those things, too. But she wished she could make him see that there was so much more. "Is that...all?"

Erik was as uncomfortable with the conversation as he was with his physical state. It was grossly unfair that the same woman who could arouse him with a look, a word, a touch, was a hopeless romantic who would probably be shocked at the steamy scenarios between the two of them that had become an integral part of his thoughts. She was wasting her life waiting for her true love. And the best in Erik, the unselfish part of him, wished he could convince her otherwise. He hated to see her channeling all that unspent passion into useless dreams of "someday."

"I don't believe in romantic love, Julie," he said firmly. "I don't believe in a woman finding her prince and being swept off to live happily ever after with him. It doesn't happen that way in real life."

"It could, if the prince would let it," she said, sounding a little wistful. That made Erik irritable.

"If he's really a prince, he'll attend to his duty," he grumbled. "Everyone's better off that way, and no one gets hurt by any illusions of love." His own clear-cut sense of duty got cloudy whenever he got too close to Julie. From now on he would keep his distance.

He led her off the dance floor. "I've had enough of this," he said. "Let's get out of here."

Julie felt him pull away from her, robbing her of the warm feeling of protection he had enveloped her in while dancing. She was left with nothing to hold on to but the feeling that although her dream was as real as a rainbow, a shooting star or a moonbeam, it was just as elusive.

Chapter Seven

Julie would have to have been the most insensitive person on earth not to notice the change in Erik after that night. He was unfailingly polite and considerate, but distant. Gone was the easy camaraderie which had built up between them during the weeks before. Gone were the faint glimmers of caring that she had begun to discern in him. Gone were the casual touches that had had a far from casual effect on her.

She missed them. She missed *him*. He might as well not have been there. But sensing that he needed solitude just then, and respecting his right to it, she did nothing. Except wait.

As agreed, Drew dropped Lexi off at the castle early on Monday morning. Julie was glad for the diversion. A day with Lexi would be anything but boring.

She arrived in full princess regalia, holding up the front of her long gown so that she wouldn't trip going up the front stairs. Balancing on her blond head was a homemade crown of construction paper and glitter.

Waiting at the door with Erik, Julie received her as an honored guest. "So nice that you could manage a visit with us, Princess Lexi. We hope you will enjoy your stay."

"I'm certain I shall, Prince Erik and Princess Julie," Lexi said, making her six-year-old voice as dignified as possible. She curtsied to them both, then added in a breathless aside, "It's okay if I call you Princess Julie, isn't it? I mean, you will be, after you're married."

Erik, who had seemed captivated at first, turned away at Lexi's reference to their marriage. Julie forced a smile and answered Lexi, "It's fine. After all, I'm as much a princess as you are, sweetie."

Lexi was awed by the castle, despite the many visits to Julie she had made there over the past year. With Rufus following behind her, she disappeared for half the morning, exploring every nook and cranny she could find. From time to time she returned to Julie or Erik, whichever one she found first, with delighted reports of places she was sure would be good hiding places for treasure, or which might be the entrance to a secret passage.

Her enthusiasm was infectious, and Julie noticed that before long, Erik was sharing with her his own boyhood beliefs about the castle's secrets. With Julie's permission, they "explored" her room in the tower, which had been his bedroom as a boy.

Julie was coming up the stairs with some laundry when she heard Lexi ask him, "Can you see Isle Anders from way up here?"

"I can," he answered.

"Really?" she asked, peering out across the ocean.

"Not like some people consider *really*," he answered truthfully. "But in my mind, when I look across the ocean, over that way," he said, pointing, "I can just picture it the way it looked when I last saw it," she asked.

Lexi was a perceptive little girl.

"It's my home," he answered simply. When he noticed Julie had entered the room, he changed the subject. "I was just going to ask Lexi if she'd like to go outside to play with Rufus," he told her.

"Yes, yes!" Lexi shouted.

"Sure," Julie said. "I'll get some refreshments ready while you're out there." She turned to Lexi. "Would you do us the honor of joining us for tea, Princess Lexi?"

"The honor is mine," Lexi said gravely. Julie was sure that Erik found Lexi's manners and precociousness as enchanting as she did. But when she made eye contact with him on the way out, to share her delight, he gave her no more than a polite nod.

As she had promised, Julie set up their lunch as if it were a formal tea. Every time she looked out onto the lawn, she saw that not only were Rufus and Lexi involved in a game of chase, but that Erik joined in also. Relaxed, smiling, he looked like he was enjoying himself thoroughly. Children, it seemed, were indeed one of his soft spots. Like animals were. And that was at least a start.

Later, sitting around the table, all three of them used their most formal manners.

"Delectable, utterly delectable," Lexi declared after biting into her grilled cheese sandwich. "Your cook is a jewel."

"I'll pass along your compliments, Your Highness," Julie said. She turned to Erik. "Would you like seconds, Prince Erik? You must have worked up an appetite out there.''

''Thank you,'' Erik said politely, but he refrained from calling her Princess Julie.

Lexi looked back and forth between the two of them, and dropped the formality abruptly. ''Are you in love with Julie?'' she asked Erik.

Erik was momentarily taken aback. No one had ever asked him that, point-blank, before. While he was searching for an answer that would satisfy his need for honesty while not tipping off Lexi to the truth, she spoke again.

''I mean, you're always looking at her when you think she's not looking and all that,'' Lexi said. ''But,'' she added, frowning. ''You haven't kissed her once all day.''

He hadn't kissed her, to be precise, for one and one half days, since the dinner in Boston. He had stayed out of the public eye since then, for that very reason. He hadn't thought they'd have to show affection in front of a child to be believable as an engaged couple, but it seemed that now his bluff had been called.

''I haven't?'' he said, sounding surprised. ''Then I will have to remedy that, won't I?'' And with that he went over to Julie and gave her a kiss on the lips.

Julie, despite the fact that she was chewing a mouthful of grilled cheese sandwich, felt a pleasant jolt at the familiar contact of his lips. Irked at feeling gratified by this cursory attention, when she should have felt insulted at his noticeable lack of attention, she used the ringing phone as a welcome way to hide her flushed face. She made it to the kitchen and got it on the fourth ring, after tripping over Rufus, who was looking for handouts as usual.

It was the animal shelter, calling for Erik. She handed the phone to him and went back out to the table with Lexi.

A few minutes later he came back into the dining room. "Someone's come to claim Rufus," he said, avoiding Julie's eyes. "I've got to take him right over to the shelter. They're waiting."

While Erik went to get his car keys, Lexi lavished hugs on the dog. Rufus, still with one eye on the remains of their lunch, was amenable to the attention, though uncomprehending of its meaning. When Erik returned, Lexi said, "I bet he's going to miss you." She sniffed. "Why can't you keep him?"

Erik knelt down and looked her in the eye. His voice was gentle. "His owners are thrilled that they've finally found him, Lexi. He strayed from their campsite twenty miles from here, and the whole family has been worried sick about him, especially the little boy. Rufus will be so happy to see them again, he'll never miss me."

"But you'll miss him." It wasn't a question, but it was.

Erik patted her on the shoulder. "Yes, princess," he said huskily. "I'll miss him, all right."

Julie watched him leave. It was no mystery why he avoided love. Too many times for him, loving meant losing.

Once the lunch dishes were cleaned up, Lexi said, "Julie, let's make up a fairy tale."

It was their custom to invent a tale together. Usually one of them set up the scene and posed the problem, and the other one finished it. Julie, who was always amazed at Lexi's imagination, loved doing this as much as Lexi did. The idea might be educational, but more importantly, it was fun.

"Let's go up to the tower," Julie suggested. It wouldn't hurt to have Lexi lie down and rest, after she had been running around all day. They lay side by side on her bed on their stomachs, chins propped on their fists, looking out of the window and across the sea.

Julie took a deep breath, trying to clear her mind of all that had been troubling her, and began. "Once upon a time," she said, "there was a prince."

"Was he handsome?" Lexi asked, in what was sure to be the first of many interruptions.

"Is that important?"

Lexi wrinkled her forehead. "No, not really. But is he nice?"

"Yes. And strong and loyal and...devoted to duty."

Lexi's eyes widened. "You mean what Rufus does on the lawn?"

Julie laughed. "No. Devoted to duty means that he does what he is supposed to do."

"Oh. You mean like fight dragons, rescue maidens and all that prince stuff?"

"He did everything that was his duty," Julie said.

"Like your prince does?"

Julie knew that Lexi didn't suspect who the story was really about. "Yes," she said.

"What else about the prince?"

Julie thought for a moment. "There was a spell on him."

Lexi's eyes widened. "Was he turned into a frog?"

"No. His heart was frozen. He couldn't fall in love."

"Oh, the poor prince. He must not have been happy."

"He thought he was. He only wanted one thing."

"What?"

"A bride."

"Why?" Lexi asked, puzzled. "If he couldn't fall in love."

Lexi was getting into the story now, and so was she, Julie realized. "Because getting married was his duty," she explained.

"Oh. He *has* to do it."

"Exactly."

"Not like Prince Erik. He *wants* to marry you, Julie."

Julie gazed out over the restless ocean, lost in thoughts that Lexi finally interrupted. "What happened next, Julie?"

"There was a woman."

"Pretty?"

"Does it matter?"

"No. But was she a princess?" Lexi asked hopefully.

"No."

Lexi thought about that for a minute. "She wasn't a princess on the outside," she said decidedly. "But she was a princess on the inside. And the inside is the important part, right, Julie?"

"Right," Julie said with a smile. "Anyway, this woman agreed to be the prince's bride."

"Why, if he didn't love her?"

"She knew he needed her help."

"She must have loved him."

Julie gave a wistful smile. "More than anything," she said.

"Was she happy?"

"She was happy to be helping him," Julie said

slowly. "But she wanted him to be happy, and she knew he wasn't."

"He'd be happy if he fell in love with her," Lexi said. "Wouldn't he?"

"She thinks so."

"Well, then she has to break the spell."

"You're right, Lexi." If only it were that easy. "How?"

"She doesn't know how," Julie admitted.

"Oh, no," Lexi said, distress in her voice. "It can't end there. We need a happy ending."

They were silent for a few minutes, both thinking. Suddenly Lexi jumped up.

"I know how!" she shouted. She knelt on the bed, facing Julie, and spoke excitedly. "His heart is frozen, so she has to melt it."

"How?"

"Well..." Lexi said, her brows knit in concentration. After a while her face lit up. "I know. She hugs him a real long time, and all the warm love in her heart spills over into his and melts it, and then he falls in love with her."

It was simple, but Julie had to admit it made perfect sense. "Sounds like a great ending to me."

"That's not the end!"

"It isn't?"

"No, of course not, silly," Lexi said, giggling. "We can't forget the part about then they lived happily ever after. The end." She smiled so triumphantly that Julie couldn't help laughing.

She gave Lexi a hug. "Now *that's* what I call a great ending," she said.

Erik still hadn't returned by the time Drew came to pick Lexi up at the end of the day. That didn't surprise

Julie. He would have needed time alone after leaving Rufus, even if he hadn't been in such a distant mood lately.

But she was restless all alone in the castle, and she didn't want him to think she was waiting around for him. So she left him a note and went into town to see Annah.

Annah had just closed her secondhand shop. Julie helped her straighten up while telling her about the day with Lexi. Annah made her laugh with a story of a particularly demanding customer she'd had that day, but then Julie became lost in her own thoughts as she hung clothing back on the racks.

Annah's voice was gentle. "Julie, do you want to talk about it?"

Julie snapped out of her reverie. "About what?"

Annah scanned her face. "Oh, I don't know. The something important that's on your mind. The thing that's bothering you."

"There's nothing bothering me," Julie said, immediately contradicting herself by adding, "Anyway, it's not important."

Annah sat down and gave Julie a probing look. "Not important?" she said. "When one of my two best friends falls in love, I call that important."

Annah would know, of course. She had the gift. With something like relief, Julie sat down next to her and heaved a sigh.

"Want to talk about it?"

"Yes, I think I would," Julie said. She couldn't tell Annah everything, of course, but it would feel wonderful to share some of it with a friend who cared. Annah went out front and got them both a tall iced coffee, then sat down again. "When did this happen?" she asked.

"The night of the ball, as far as everyone in the world except you believes," Julie said with a wistful smile. "But I talked you into thinking that your true-love instinct was off."

"It could have been," Annah said, shrugging.

Julie hugged her impulsively. "The world is full of people who think they're never wrong," she said. "Thank you for not being one of them."

"So I was right," Annah mused. "You weren't in love when you got engaged to Erik."

"You must be wondering why I did it."

"I'm sure you had a good reason, but please, don't tell me," Annah said. "I don't need to know. And that's not what concerns me, anyway."

Julie relaxed a little more. She had known all along she wouldn't betray Erik; she couldn't tell her friend that the engagement wasn't real. But it was a relief to know that Annah didn't want to know their secret. "You are the most accepting person I know. I can't believe some guy hasn't snapped you up."

Annah shook her head. "You're something else, Julie. I may be able to spot true love, but you have such incredible faith in it. You probably think some prince will come along for me, too."

"When one does, at least you'll know if he loves you," Julie said ruefully.

"Ah, so that's it. You're in love with your fiancé, but your problem is you don't know whether he is in love with you."

"He hasn't given me much reason to think he is," Julie admitted. "Although Erik isn't an easy person to read."

"He was that first morning, after the ball." Julie rolled her eyes. "No kidding. No, I *know* he wasn't in love with me then. But since, there have been times when I wondered if maybe..." Her voice trailed off.

When Annah spoke again, her voice was heavy. "Julie, do you want me to use my insight for you? Do you want me to tell you whether Erik is in love with you or not?"

"You know, don't you?"

Annah sighed. "I think so. Although, as you said, Erik is not an easy person to read. But my feeling's been getting stronger lately."

Julie had been getting stronger cues lately, too, and they had all pointed toward Erik's withdrawal from her. It was clear that Annah didn't want to share what she knew with Julie, and there could be only one reason for that. Julie squared her shoulders and shook her head.

"No," she said. "Don't tell me. I'm better off not knowing. If Erik does love me, how wonderful it will be when he reveals it, in his own time and his own way." With a shaky smile, she added, "And if he doesn't, I don't want to know because I don't want to give up hope that he still may come to love me in the future."

Now it was Annah's turn to give a hug. "You're amazing, do you know that? I don't know how many other people who would choose to look away from a crystal ball."

"Thank you for offering to share your gift, anyway."

"I haven't decided whether it's a gift or a curse," Annah said with a little smile.

"Funny, I was thinking the same thing about my loving Erik."

Annah turned serious again. "I just hope he knows how privileged he is to have earned your love."

"I'll make sure he does, whether he ever loves me back or not," Julie said lightly. She stood up. "C'mon," she said, pulling Annah to her feet. "Let's go get some supper."

Erik was back when she got home to the castle, holed up in the library, apparently doing some paperwork. It wasn't late, but Julie decided to go up to her room in the tower.

Brushing her hair, she looked out at the dark sky and the darker ocean. Through the open windows she could hear the ocean swishing around the rocks below and then whispering away again. Swishing, whispering. Again, again. It was calming, the ceaseless motion of the sea, and exciting. How she had missed it when she had lived in the city. No matter where the future took her, she hoped she would always be able to live near the ocean.

She put down the brush, but was feeling too restless to go to bed so early. Instead, she decided to go outside for a while. She slipped down the back staircase and out the kitchen door, and, without even thinking about it, headed for the secluded place at the edge of the bluff that was still her secret spot.

Pushing through the tangled woods and into the clearing, she paused to look out at the view spread before her. Suddenly a voice spoke to her from behind.

"History repeats itself."

She turned around and saw Erik step from the shadows. She didn't think he even remembered this place where they had once met so long ago it seemed like a dream. "I came out here a little while ago."

"Oh," Julie said. She paused, feeling awkward.

There she stood in the darkness, face-to-face with the man she loved. It was the most natural thing in the world to want to step into his arms, to offer comfort for the pain that had brought him out there and to receive comfort for the uncertainty that had brought her. But his voice, his face, his stance were unreceptive. As if his heart were frozen indeed.

A memory of Lexi, on her bed that afternoon, flashed through Julie's mind. *She hugs him a real long time, and all the warm love in her heart spills over into his...*

Before her next heartbeat, she was in his arms. She said nothing, just held him, her arms wrapped tightly around his solid body, her face buried in his chest. Just held him and hoped her warmth would melt him.

He was evidently surprised at first and definitely unreceptive. Stiff and unbending, he linked his arms around her loosely, probably for the sake of balance. But he didn't push her away, so she stayed where she was, running her hands along his back, willing him to soften, to yield. She knew he was attracted to her physically. And that attraction just might prove to be the one chink in his armor, the one way she could get through to him and tap into the feelings that she sensed were there underneath all that self-control. If so, she wasn't above using it. Her instincts told her that, for him, an emotional commitment might follow a physical one.

She stood on tiptoe and knew that he must feel the friction between their bodies as keenly as she did. Wrapping her arms around the back of his neck, she felt her breasts flatten against him. She buried her face against his neck and pressed her lips to the smooth skin just below his ear. "Erik," she whispered softly.

Her warm breath on his ear as she said his name was his undoing. He tightened his hold on her, and her shivered response stripped away another layer of his self-control. Then she lifted her head from his shoulder, and he felt the dewy warmth of her lips next to his; and time paused as she stayed there, waiting, offering herself to him as she had that night nine years before.

But this time it was more than he could withstand. He crushed his lips against hers, eating at their ripe tenderness. When they were slicker and hotter than he could bear, his tongue plunged inside her mouth. She accepted it willingly—no, eagerly—and joined him in a mutual exploration that took him to a place in passion where he had never been before. They were perfectly attuned, their bodies straining and shifting and realigning with an instinctive mutual grace that practice and design could never match. And something within told him that this dance would move only in one direction. As inevitably as the sun would rise again over the ocean that roared below them, he would be her lover.

She felt his body surrender, and joy hummed through her, a sweet counterpoint to passion. She had more than melted him; he was on fire, his kiss white-hot in its sheer intensity. She had never before felt the full force of his attention concentrated on her, but she felt it now with every fiber of her being. The reserve, the control that she had always admired in him were stronger than she had imagined, to have held such awesome power in check. His kiss was both masterful and yielding. He welcomed her advances no less than he pressed for his own, which made her realize that she wielded a power of her own. It was a uniquely feminine power, and it came coupled with a feminine need that made her ache. When he broke off the kiss momentarily to heave in great gulps of the salt air, her need escaped in a little moan of frustration.

He was far too masculine not to pick up on that, and the next thing she knew, he had lifted her in his arms. After a few quick, hard kisses he laid her down on the ground and stretched out next to her. He propped himself up on one elbow, and his free hand roamed her body along with his eyes. There was fire in them, and it flared when he raised the hem of her shirt and pushed it up past her breasts. Julie felt her body flush under the appreciation she felt in that ardent gaze, and the raw yearning. He looked his fill, unselfconsciously, while he palmed the smooth, sensitive skin of her belly, stoking the growing need in her. When she didn't think she could stand any more of this measured caress, at last he rolled toward her, anchoring one leg over her and bringing his mouth down on hers for another demanding kiss.

This time, while she matched the wild insistence of his tongue, she felt his hand glide up until it covered one breast. With sure, deliberately teasing strokes, he kneaded and measured it, molding and reshaping until she bucked in protest. Knowing better than she did what she was asking for, he at last paid attention to the sensitive nub in the center, plucking it gently with his fingertips until it stood up hard against his palm. She was lost in a sea of sensation, defined for that moment in time by the consuming touch of the man she loved.

For the second time he broke off a kiss that had nearly overridden his body's need for oxygen. His breathing was ragged, his heart pounded blood through him in a rhythm that echoed the insistent pounding of the ocean against the rocks below. He shifted uncomfortably, realizing that the urgency of his desire was becoming difficult to ignore. Beneath him the woman who was taking him to unknown heights of pleasure writhed at his slightest touch, which only sent him rocketing higher. The signals she was sending were too clear for him to mistake, but he had to be sure.

"Julie?" he asked, and his voice sounded rough around the edges.

"Yes?" she whispered, her eyes focusing on his.

"Do you want me to make love to you?"

"Yes," she whispered, urgently this time. It was a clear mandate, her words punctuated by her arms, which wrapped around him and tried to pull him down on top of her. Muscles tense, he resisted, knowing the kind of woman she was. He searched her eyes for any sign of doubt, but saw none.

"Are you sure?" he asked, offering her a last chance to change her mind.

She couldn't understand his hesitation. "Of course I'm sure," she said. And suddenly, in her need to convince him, she blurted out, "Erik, I *love* you."

He didn't move a muscle; he remained poised above her, his muscles locked in a battle against gravity and against instinct. But somehow she knew that her words had struck bone-deep. Slowly he straightened and sat up next to her, staring out at the ocean. And at his withdrawal, the chill of disappointment crept insidiously inside her.

Erik breathed deeply, struggling to regain the control he had lost. If he hadn't let his lust run away with his thinking, he would have realized that a woman like Julie wouldn't give herself to a man unless she loved him. This was his fault. He'd had a duty to her, because he had asked her to be his damned fiancée in the first place, and he hadn't done it. He should have stayed away from her, but he hadn't. Now she had real feelings for him. And real feelings led to real hurt. He had never, ever meant to hurt her.

Julie sat up next to him and yanked down her shirt. She was *furious!* Not only had she spilled her guts to him—again—but also he had pulled away from her again. Not only that, but she had never been more aroused in her life. And he had the nerve to sit there looking so darn calm! She was hot and uncomfortable and so angry she couldn't speak.

"This has gone too far," he said.

"Wrong," she spat out. It had not gone far enough, not nearly.

"I never meant for you to love me."

"Tough," she said. "It happens sometimes. It's not like I could help it."

"Are you sure?"

Her eyes narrowed. "What is that supposed to mean?"

"I can't help wondering if you set yourself up for it," he said evenly. "You're in a fairy-tale world, living in that tower and believing in true love just like you did when you were sixteen."

That did it. Julie jumped to her feet and planted her hands on her hips, glaring down at him. "How *dare* you pass judgment on me like that! Yes, I still believe in love, but I believe in it because it's real. I loved you when I was sixteen, I love you now and, God help me, I loved you all that time in between. How could I *not* believe in love?"

She was on a roll now, and nothing was going to

stop her until she had said her fill. "Listen, Your Highness, I might live in the tower of a castle now, but I worked a lot of years in the inner city. You don't get more real than that. I've seen children wasting away for lack of love, grasping for it like drowning men grasp for straws and somehow miraculously staying afloat with the little that comes their way from teachers and other people who care. I've seen couples in the depths of poverty whose lives have hope and dignity because of the love they share with each other and their children," she said, her voice impassioned. "So don't accuse me of living in a fairy tale, Prince Erik. I believe in love because, from what I've seen with my own eyes and felt with my own heart, it is the only thing that can bring happiness, peace and meaning to life. It's real, all right, and what's more, it's the only thing that matters."

Her chest heaved as she caught her breath. "I don't take love lightly, mister. So when I tell someone I love them, they'd better sit up and take notice." She pointed at him, adding, "And I love *you*, Erik Anders."

The sound of her voice echoing off the rocks gradually died away. Exhausted by her tirade and by her unspent passion, Julie wrapped her arms around herself, shivering in the night air that seemed suddenly to have thrown a chill over the world. "I—I'm going for a walk," she said, and turned away.

Erik sat where he was for some time after she left. Then he got up and made his way to the castle, wondering how long it would take him to pack up and get out of there.

He was just about to get out his suitcases when there was a knock on his door. "Erik," Julie said, sounding a little breathless. "Are you in there?"

"Yes," he said. He knew he'd have to talk to her before he left, and now was as good a time as any.

"Come in."

Before he finished speaking, she burst into his room. Her face was white. He couldn't help feeling alarmed.

"Julie," he said. "What's the matter?"

She spoke rapidly. "He's just arrived. He called to tell us he was on his way when we were both out this afternoon, but neither one of us checked for messages. He's downstairs."

"Who is?"

"Your father," she said, her eyebrows drawn down with concern. "And Erik—he doesn't look good."

Chapter Eight

The king didn't look good, and it was no wonder. After he went to bed, Gustave, who had accompanied him on the trip, filled Erik and Julie in on the details.

King Ivar's doctor had discharged him early that morning, and the king had been determined to follow through on his intention to visit them at the castle at Anders Point, before returning to Maine. He had insisted on traveling to Maine by car instead of flying; he didn't like air travel, and he would have to go by plane when he made the trip to Isle Anders.

It was by no means a short drive to begin with, but problems with traffic and with the limo's engine had prolonged the journey. As he had bidden them good-night, the king had insisted that he felt fine, that he was only tired, and Gustave was inclined to agree with him.

"The doctor kept him under observation far longer than normal," he reminded them. "When he discharged him, he was convinced that the king's recovery had progressed to the point that he would be ready for such travel. I think you will see a marked improvement in him after he has had the rest he needs.'' Then he, too, retired for the night.

Julie went upstairs, as well. She finished using the bathroom that she shared with Erik, then started toward the archway that led to her room in the tower.

Erik was standing at his bedroom window, staring out. ''I'm sorry,'' he said quietly.

She didn't answer, but she stopped and stood behind him.

''I'm sorry you fell in love with me, Julie. I never meant you to.''

''I know,'' she said softly. All he had wanted was a pretend fiancée.

He turned around to face her. ''What can I do to make you stop?''

Soft laughter rippled up from inside her. ''There's nothing you can do,'' she said. ''Erik, you might rule a country, but you can't rule my heart.''

He was silent for a few minutes, and then he spoke again. ''Julie, I want you to know that I'm going to end this engagement as soon as possible.''

''What about your father?''

''He'll leave for Isle Anders soon. And when he goes, I'll go, too. That will be a good time to break this off,'' he said briskly. ''Then you can resume your own life, and everything will get back to the way it should be.''

Julie shook her head. What irony, that the same hidden vulnerability that was part of what drew her to him was keeping him from getting close to her. ''Erik, running away from my love won't make it go away. I'll love you wherever you are.''

''I think time and distance will change your mind.''

"No, you don't. You only *hope* so. I think that deep down you believe in love as much as I do."

His expression turned grim. "If you think that, then you haven't been paying attention."

"I've been paying enough attention to realize that you think it will hurt less to be the one who leaves than the one who loses," she said softly. "It would be too risky for you to admit that I might be right, and stay to find out."

He looked at her. "Julie, after what just happened outside, you know as well as I do what would happen if I stayed here with you."

"Yes."

He swore under his breath. "If I were a certain kind of man, I'd stay here and tell you lies and take advantage of your affection for me," he said through gritted teeth. "But I'm trying to do what's right, whether you like it or not."

She shook her head and sighed. "Go ahead, Erik. Be noble. Do whatever you think is your duty," she said. "But that won't change the fact that I'm in love with you, whether *you* like it or not." And with that she turned away and went up the stairs.

Erik might have wanted a quick getaway, but it was not to be. Although his father looked better, he still tired easily and spent most of the next day lying down. On the following day, he divided his time between playing chess with Gustave in the library and sitting in a lounge chair on the side lawn, talking to Julie. The day after that, Erik drove him to Anders Point. The king enjoyed seeing old familiar places and faces immensely, but he spent the rest of the day in his room, resting.

Erik's hands were tied, and he hated that feeling. Not only was he anxious to get away from this agonizing limbo he was in with Julie, but he was also concerned that the king might not be doing as well as his doctor had thought. As a result he spent a lot of his waking hours, and there were more of them than usual, pacing. But on the fourth day his father seemed more his old self, and when the doctor came to the castle that morning to give him a checkup, he pronounced the king in fine health.

But just when Erik's concerns about his father eased, the situation with Julie worsened. Full of his customary air of command again, the king began to take a very active interest in their engagement. At lunch he asked them, with deceptive casualness, "How are the wedding plans going?"

Erik was at a loss as to how to field a question like that. As he hesitated, Julie stepped in and answered.

"Your Majesty, it's still early. We're in the negotiation stage," she said, giving Erik a meaningful look.

"Negotiating the details for the wedding? Good, good," said the king. "Although if I were you, son, I'd put my trust in your bride-to-be. Women know best about these things."

Still looking at Erik, Julie lifted her eyebrows pointedly. He turned to his father. "As Julie said, it's a little early to worry about wedding plans. We just got engaged, sire."

The king ignored him. "Give him time, my dear," he said to Julie, chuckling. "If what I saw in my closet at the hospital is any indication, it won't take long before he's begging you to speed up the process. And in the meantime, let's take a little walk so you can tell me your ideas for the wedding." He pushed his chair back and got up from the table.

"Uh—of course," Julie said, glancing at Erik as she stood up.

The king, who was already walking away, looked back at Erik. "You will join us, of course."

Erik joined them in the physical sense only, and only loosely in that regard. He kept several paces behind as Julie strolled out of the dining room with the king. He spoke not at all, and the look of concentration on his face seemed to be focused somewhere far off.

That left Julie on her own to focus on the king and try to sound coherent. Of course, there were no wedding plans; not one. The easiest thing to do when he asked her questions, therefore, was simply to describe her dream wedding.

"Would you like the ceremony to take place here, or on Isle Anders?" the king began.

"For as long as I can remember, I've always wanted to be married right here, in this castle," she answered truthfully. "Where you married Queen Alexandra."

The king seemed pleased. "The ballroom is a splendid setting," he said heartily. "Neither too large nor too small—"

"And the lighting is heavenly in there in the afternoon," Julie added, warming to the topic.

"Let's go in and take a look, shall we?"

They did, and he agreed with her observation. He checked his watch. "Two o'clock on the dot," he observed. "A fine time for the ceremony to begin."

Julie glanced at Erik, but saw no indication that he was paying any attention whatever. "Two o'clock sounds perfect," she agreed.

"What about music? Would you like a full orchestra, off to the side?" the king asked.

Julie thought about that. "I'd be partial to a string quartet for the ceremony, to be joined by a small orchestra afterward for the reception."

"Sounds fine. How extensive would you like the guest list to be?"

"I'd like to keep it small and personal. Family and close friends."

The king nodded approvingly. "Once you get beyond that, the sheer numbers would be staggering. One of the disadvantages of marrying into royalty, you know." He took her left hand. "And the wedding band, I suppose, would match your engagement ring. Unless you'd prefer something different."

"Oh, no. I love this ring," she said, looking down at the blue stone on her left hand. She knew now that Erik *had* chosen it for her, as he had told the king. His friend Lucas had told her that Erik had ordered an emerald the morning of the ball, but had called to switch to a sapphire after the announcement. It may have been simply to blot any memory of Roberta and her betrayal, but still, it made the ring special to Julie.

"What about a wedding gown?"

"My mother's," Julie said succinctly. Then she frowned and added, "Unless it wouldn't be fancy enough."

Looking pleased, the king assured her that would not be the case. "This is your day. No protocol outrules your wishes. And I happen to be quite fond of tradition myself. Now, about flowers. Spare no expense, my dear. You could carry an armful of red roses, and we could have dozens more along the——"

Julie shook her head.

"No?" the king said, stopping. "What, then?"

"Daisies. They're my favorites. I'm afraid I'm a simple girl at heart, Your Majesty."

He tucked her arm in his and chuckled. "My son is luckier than he knows," he said, loud enough for Erik to hear—if he had been listening. "Now, my dear, as for the menu," he said, steering her toward the kitchen, where Gustave was cleaning up after lunch.

She smiled. "That's easy," she said. "The menu is anything Gustave thinks would be best. After what he did at the ball, I trust him implicitly."

The king's smile widened. "After that endorsement, I'll give him a raise," he said. "Or else I'll let him best me in a game of chess, whichever would give him the most satisfaction."

"So that's all there is to the wedding I've always dreamed of," Julie said, hoping to redirect the king's attention. "Everything taken care of."

The king chuckled. "No, no, my dear. You are forgetting something."

"I am?" Julie ticked off a mental checklist. Food, flowers, music, guests, rings, gown, setting....

"Yes, indeed. You can't get married without a license."

"Oh, well that's not—"

"And the blood tests, of course," he added.

Julie gave Erik a look of sheer panic. His face showed no emotion, but she knew he wasn't happy about having to drive into town to take care of such business. But the king had left them no choice. In fact, he went along with them, talking happily with the townspeople they met in the process.

"You are more than a good sport to humor him like this," Erik whispered to Julie at the first opportunity. "Just remember, this doesn't mean a thing."

"Easy for you to say," she grumbled. "Just be ready to catch me. I've been known to pass out at the sight of a sewing needle."

When they got back to the castle, Erik decided it was time to put the brakes on his father's enthusiasm. But he would have to apply them gently.

"I'm glad that's finished. You could get married at any time, now," the king said with satisfaction as they entered the kitchen door.

"Your Majesty," Erik began. "I feel it is imperative that I remind you that Julie and I have only recently gotten engaged. A hasty wedding was never part of our plans," he said truthfully. "And, of course, I don't need to be married before my coronation. I understand the concern you had in the hospital. But now that you've recovered, I'm sure you'll see there is no reason to rush."

"The point is that you're all set. All systems are go." He winked at Gustave, who was sitting at the table. Gustave shook his head, chuckling, and went back to looking through a stack of low-fat recipes he was trying out on the king.

That night at dinner King Ivar said unexpectedly, "Gustave and I will leave tomorrow for Isle Anders."

That bit of welcome news gave Erik's spirits a much needed boost. He was glad to put an end to the nerve-racking charade that the day had been.

Just as unexpectedly his father added, "And I would like you to accompany me to Isle Anders, my son, to resume your former duties. You have been away long enough."

Erik couldn't believe his good luck. This was what he had been hoping for all along—his father nearly recovered and in good spirits, and himself back where he wanted to be, doing what he wanted to do. This engagement of his had done what he had wanted, and the best part was it would soon be over. He'd be across the Atlantic in Isle Anders, and Julie would stay here at the Point, too far away to be a temptation to him any longer.

But Erik's relief was short-lived. To his dismay, the king turned next to Julie and said, "I assume, of course, that you will be coming with Erik. In fact, I insist on it."

"Actually—" Erik began.

But Julie shot him a look across the table that stopped him. He knew what that look was saying, and to his chagrin, he knew she was right. The king was improving, but far from robust. It was clear that his mind was made up on this; he would not take no for an answer, and arguing with him would only cause undue distress and, maybe, suspicion. They had started this thing, and now they had to see it through.

Like him, Julie Britton knew her duty and did it. It was one of the things he liked about her. It was one of the things he would miss when this was over.

Like the sound of her laughter. And the sight of a rosy blush dawning in her cheeks. The bite of her anger and the warmth of her caress. And the taste of her—

He pulled himself from his reverie to find both Julie and his father looking at him expectantly. He swallowed. "Actually," he began again, "I think Julie will enjoy Isle Anders." It wouldn't be so bad, he told himself. He would be engrossed in his work, after all. They could lie low for a few days until his father's attention had turned elsewhere and then invent some reason for her to have to return to Maine.

"Splendid," the king said, rubbing his hands together. "Then it's all settled. And I have hereby decided that precisely one week from tomorrow, it will be my privilege to host the country's traditional betrothal feast in your honor."

For Julie the trip to Isle Anders was her last hope to get through to Erik. They both needed to get away from the castle at Anders Point for a while. She hoped that getting back to his home element would help him see their relationship in a whole new light, and maybe bring to light the feelings she hoped he had for her, underneath his protective layer of duty. If it didn't, she knew deep down that once she left Isle Anders it would be the end of her connection to Erik.

But seeing Erik in his element gave her new insight into him. It happened gradually throughout the week. Observing him at work, she realized the importance of his position. The welfare of many people depended on his doing his duty. As they traveled around the island sight-seeing, she saw more than the breathtaking scenery of his jewel of a homeland. She saw the spirit and loyalty of the people, their sense of connection to him and his to them. He was accessible, he was respected, and more, he was loved. It was obvious in the freedom with which they voiced their opinions and the heartiness of their congratulations. Never had Julie felt worse about the false engagement.

By the end of the week she began to wonder how she was going to make it through the betrothal feast the king had planned. She had learned that such a feast had long been a tradition on Isle Anders, and every citizen was invited to attend. In her room in the palace she dressed for the occasion with resignation and a vague sense of dread.

The feast was to be held outdoors on the palace grounds, and the turnout was tremendous. It had been a long time since the one for King Ivar, and Erik had been of marriageable age for so long that the anticipation of this event had been building for quite some time.

Alone in his room Erik watched out his window as the crowd swelled. Before long it would be time for him to get Julie and escort her to the feast.

Everything would go smoothly, he knew. He had absolute confidence that Julie would do her part and do it well. Time after time since the start of their partnership at the ball, her loyalty had been put to the test, and time after time she had come through for him. Even after she had told him she loved him and he had rejected her, she had stuck by her original promise and was still keeping up appearances for his sake; for the sake of the king. There was probably not another woman in the world who would do that, and Erik knew it.

Other than her insistence that she loved him, the only problem in their partnership as far as he could tell was their mutual physical attraction. That made it hard for him to focus on his duty, although he had to admit that it had certainly helped make the engagement look real, especially to the king. That was a surprise to Erik. His father had always been so distant and cool in their own relationship, it seemed strange for him to seem so pleased with Erik and Julie's outward affection. Since the night he had come so dangerously close to over-stepping his boundaries with Julie, touching her had become especially challenging to Erik; challenging to stop, anyway. To a man like him, who prided himself on his ability to be detached and clear thinking, this intense physical attraction was a definite drawback.

When he knocked on her door, Julie was ready. She was wearing a long, flowing gown of the same color blue as the one she had worn to the ball, the sapphire blue of her eyes. But there were troubled shadows in those eyes as he tucked her arm in his.

"Ready?" he said huskily, giving her hand a gentle squeeze. She nodded, but he didn't start walking.

"Nervous?" he asked gently.

She nodded again, but gave him a trembling smile this time. What a woman! He was proud to appear before his countrymen with her. She was far more suited to this than Roberta would have been, and—

The errant thought stopped him cold. It was true. He had chosen Julie as his pretend fiancée; but she would have been a better choice for his real fiancée. Distinctly uncomfortable with that thought, he banished it and escorted Julie out to the balcony of his father's room, where they were met with thunderous applause by the crowd on the lawn.

After that traditional, formal appearance, they went outside and mingled with the guests. The good wishes of the people deeply affected Erik. He hadn't foreseen how adept his pretend fiancée would be at capturing hearts. He had the feeling that the folks of Isle Anders would be let down when he ended this engagement with Julie. As would his father.

As would he. His life would go back to the way it was without her. Losing all that sparkle would be sure to be a letdown. For a while, anyway. But they would all get over it, and when it was time, he would choose a real bride.

Erik had become separated from Julie now. Apart from the crowd, he leaned back against the palace wall, lost in thought. A real bride. Yes, sometime in the future, before his coronation, he would have to marry. He had always planned on choosing the woman he thought most suitable. He'd thought that was Roberta, but now he knew differently.

Julie was the woman who was most suited to be his real bride.

He probably hadn't realized it until now, because it was so simple, and right under his nose. It was perfectly logical. He watched Julie in the crowd and wondered why he hadn't seen before how ideal she was. True, she was a small-town woman, but she could handle formal social situations with aplomb. He had also wanted to marry someone whom he could count on to do her duty, and Julie had certainly proven herself trustworthy.

And now that he thought about it, their physical attraction might be a plus as well—as long as he was careful to keep on guard and not let it lead him into feelings that were too risky. Duty would be the basis of the marriage, but their attraction to each other would add another dimension. And it certainly made the business of getting heirs a lot more appealing.

"What are you doing, hiding here, big brother?"

It was Whit. Erik clapped him on the shoulder. "Just thinking about siring myself a castle full of heirs, like you once said." He smiled, feeling a weight drop off his shoulders. In one move he had solved both the problem of his false engagement and the problem of his real marriage.

"Are you planning on pulling Julie back here in the bushes and getting started right away?" Whit asked dryly.

Erik laughed. "No, little brother. I can wait." He watched Julie, talking and smiling in the crowd. "I'm going to marry that woman," he said determinedly.

Whit gave him a funny look. "I know," he said.

"We *all* know. That's why we're here."

Erik smiled and clapped him on the shoulder again. "I haven't asked you yet, so we might as well make this official. Would you be best man?"

Whit grinned. "I always was. About time you realized it," he said, dodging his brother's feigned blow. Then he turned serious. "Hey, Erik?"

Erik, who had begun to make his way over to Julie, stopped and turned back. "Yes?"

"Make sure it's real love."

It sounded odd, coming from the man they called the Prince of Hearts. Feeling his good mood start to evaporate at the mere mention of love, Erik challenged his brother. "Why?"

Whit shrugged. "You're my brother, and Julie's my old pal. I don't want either one of you to get hurt."

Erik looked at him seriously. "Neither one of us will, if I can help it," he promised.

Julie had been edgy during Erik's absence, even though he hadn't been gone all that long. She met people and talked, and smiled, but there was a hollowness inside her that seemed to suck all the pleasantness out of the evening. If she had really been Erik's fiancée, she would have felt less uncomfortable about the whole thing.

When Erik joined her there was something different about him. She didn't quite know what it was, but he seemed more relaxed than she had ever seen him in public, certainly far more relaxed than the guest of honor at a sham engagement reception should be. Although she didn't understand it, his mood had an ameliorating effect on hers: though it didn't go away, her edginess abated.

He was very attentive to her. Not just politely attentive, as he had been of late, but truly concerned with her welfare. When the crowd shifted restlessly, looking for places to sit before the program began, he put his arm around her protectively.

"How's my girl?" he murmured in her ear.

It was like it had been in the early days of their engagement. Julie applauded his timing. If ever she needed the support of someone who was on her side, it was now. She let herself relax against him as he navigated them through the crowd to the dais, where they were seated with King Ivar and Whit.

After dinner the program began. There was pomp and pageantry, singing and dancing, tradition and history. There was celebration and solemnity, and there were speeches, speeches, speeches. Most of those were in Erik's native language, and he leaned close to translate for her, murmuring in her ear in a low, sexy whisper. During the driest speech of all, Julie suddenly felt overwhelmed again. A tear escaped, and before she could wipe it away, Erik did it for her. He stopped translating, but the onlookers didn't know that, because he stayed right where he was, his arm around her, whispering reassurances in her ear. Which, somehow, made Julie want to cry all the more.

Erik thought he knew what was bothering Julie. Finally her conscience had caught up with her. She was having a hard time keeping up the pretense, here, among all this. He couldn't blame her. He would have felt the same way himself, except that he wasn't pretending anymore. To him this was their real betrothal feast, because if he had his way, they were really going to get married. On the one hand, he wanted to whisper that to her, if that would make her feel better; but on the other hand, he wasn't sure how she was going to react. It might be better to ease her into the idea because, after all, the day he would have to get married was in the distant future. Yes, that would be better. He was sure of it, given her uncertain emotional state and the fact that her reaction would be in full view of the entire citizenship of Isle Anders.

"We're coming up to the main event," he told her. "It is tradition for the current king to toast the prince and his bride-to-be. After that he'll probably say a few words, and then we're out of here. I promise. You're doing just fine, Julie."

Indeed, she had recovered her poise. She drew on some reserves from deep inside herself, and felt stronger now. Focusing on the king helped. This was for his sake.

King Ivar stepped up to the microphone. "Citizens of my beloved homeland," he began. "It is indeed a pleasure to be with you once again. Your good wishes and prayers no doubt helped to speed my recovery. For the record, I am doing just fine and plan to be a part of this community for many years to come."

He was interrupted by hearty applause. After it had died out, he said, "Thank you. But my return to good health and to your good company is not the reason for this occasion, as you all know. We are here to celebrate the betrothal of my elder son, Prince Erik. I hope you feel, as I do, that the prince has chosen his bride well."

Applause rang out again, so loud and strong as to leave no doubt about how the crowd felt about Erik's choice. When Julie's courage started to waver, she kept her eyes on King Ivar, who led the entire assembly in a toast. After the glasses had been set down once more, he spoke again.

"Tradition has chosen Prince Erik to reign as your king after me, if that is your choice also." The applause thundered out once more.

The king held up his hand for quiet. "The time for Erik's rule is near, nearer than even he knows. I felt it would be best to tell all of you at once."

At those words, dead silence reigned. Julie felt Erik stiffen next to her, and she braced herself for whatever the king was going to say.

"I will be stepping down as king before next spring. I know this news is unexpected," he added, glancing at Erik, "given that those before me have always ruled for life. I, however, knowing that I leave you in capable hands, have a great desire to enjoy a retirement. I will trade in my scepter for a fishing pole, and wish for nothing more than some grandchildren to spoil." He paused, then broke the dumbfounded silence that seemed to echo up to the sky. "My friends, this is not an occasion for sadness! Soon we will be together again for a coronation—after Erik and Julie wed and return from their honeymoon. Let us all join in celebration."

And, once the initial shock had worn off, everyone did. Except for Erik and Julie, whom no one had noticed disappearing into the side door of the palace.

Chapter Nine

Julie went willingly with Erik, glad to be away from a stressful situation that had taken an unbelievable turn for the worse.

Even working as closely with the king as she had, she had never foreseen that he would do anything but resume ruling for as long as he was physically and mentally capable of it. She'd bet the castle that Erik had been similarly taken by surprise by his father's decision to retire. Still, he remained as unflappable as ever, calmly walking her up the huge curved staircase to the second floor of the palace.

He must know, as Julie did, that the king's announcement changed everything. For her it meant the end of all hope that she would be able to win Erik over. Because now his hand was forced. In the space of precious little time, he would have to publicly break his newly celebrated engagement with her, then find another woman and marry her for real. After tonight that would seem little short of scandalous. How would it affect the king's health? Julie didn't know, but it worried her. It must be worrisome to Erik, too.

But he didn't look worried, she noticed as he led her into his bedchamber. He was a bit preoccupied now, but otherwise seemed as buoyant as he had been throughout the evening. She wondered what was on his mind, but guessed that she would soon find out. As he wished, she settled down on the sofa in the corner of his room.

She was surprised when he got down on one knee in front of her, taking her hands in his. She was even more surprised when he spoke.

"Julie, I would like to ask for your hand in marriage."

She felt her jaw drop. "You *what?*"

"I'd like to marry you."

Julie blinked, trying to dispel the fog of disbelief that had settled around her. "Are you saying you want me for your partner on a permanent basis? That if we fooled the world with a pretend engagement, we can do it with a pretend marriage? I think you're insane!"

He sat down next to her on the sofa. "No," he said quickly. "I'm not saying that at all. Our pretend engagement is over. I do want you for my partner, but for my partner in marriage, for real. I want you to be my bride."

Julie was still staring at him. She didn't say anything for a few moments, then a new thought struck her. "I don't believe this! You're using me for an escape hatch. You've got to get married fast, and here I am engaged to you. I'm the path of least resistance, all handy and convenient and available and loyal to the king and——"

"Julie, listen!" Erik interrupted her urgently. He had

never seen her like this. His Julie was like a rock, through thick and thin. He was afraid she was getting hysterical, and wondered at what point it was proper for a gentleman to douse a lady's face with cold water. In the meantime he rubbed her hands with his and spoke slowly and distinctly.

"Julie, this isn't some scheme I came up with just because my father made that announcement and I don't want to jeopardize my chance to get the crown. Give me a little credit."

After taking several deep breaths, she was able to do that. "You thought of this before his announcement?" she asked shakily.

"Yes. I decided earlier this evening."

She had no reason not to believe him. She had never, ever doubted his integrity. And it was an explanation for his odd mood change.

He swore under his breath. "I'm sorry for springing this on you so suddenly. I wasn't going to wait too long, but I was hoping you would have more time to get used to the idea."

Julie considered this. "What about you? You only thought of it a few hours ago."

He brought one of her hands to his lips. "I'm already used to the idea," he said. "In fact, I only wonder that I didn't think of it before."

"You were too busy thinking up ways to try to get rid of me," Julie reminded him.

"I said I wanted to end our false engagement," he said with a half grin. "And here's a great way to do it—replace it with a real engagement."

"I still think this has to do with convenience. Or—" She stopped, as something dawned on her. How could she forget his greatest motivating factor? "Or *duty*. Are you asking me because you know I fell in love with you, and you feel in some way responsible because you initiated our fake engagement? Well, if that's the reason, you can just forget it. I'm not in the market for any pity proposals."

"That's not it at all," Erik said soberly. "I realized this evening that you are the very best choice for a bride for me. You, Julie Britton, are a very special woman." He looked at her. "Do you want to hear why?"

"Did you actually think there was a chance I would say no to that?" she said dryly.

He grinned. "There's reason number one. Sense of humor. A woman would need that, to be married to me."

"Women need that to be married to *any* man. If we didn't have it, the institution would have died out long ago," she said. "You'd better have a better reason than that."

"I do." He turned serious again. "Julie, you have all the qualities that I have always looked for in a wife who will also be a queen. You are loyal, you are devoted to duty, you are poised and elegant. But more than that, the time we've spent together has also shown me that you care about the welfare of others, that you have your own mind and opinions and are confident enough to speak up to me, that you are wise enough to give me the distance I sometimes need and the closeness I need at other times, that you would be a wonderful mother to our children. You are very well-suited to be my wife."

It was all thought-out and well reasoned. Why should she be surprised? Erik's head ruled his heart in everything, and it was in this, too. But though she loved him, she was not about to marry him because he thought she was "suitable."

She swallowed her disappointment. Before she answered, she gave him another chance. "Is that all?" she asked.

"No," he said. "There's also this." He leaned over and kissed her. It was a hot, impatient kiss. His lips roving over hers were not asking questions, they were making demands. Demands that her body was only too willing to accede to, unless she put a stop to this. She pushed him away, and he went willingly, though not happily.

"You want to marry me because there is this—attraction between us?"

"You noticed it, too?" he asked dryly. "Hell, yes. I'd have to be crazy not to prefer to be married to a woman who, without even trying, can—" he stopped, choosing his words carefully "—elicit an impassioned response from me."

Julie didn't mince words. "Having the hots for someone is not a valid reason for marrying them, any more than your other reasons were."

"What are you saying?"

She took a deep breath. All the anger had been burned out of her. She felt only sadness, and a regret that would no doubt outlast any inconvenience she was about to cause him. "What I'm saying, Erik, is thank you very much. I'm flattered that you have asked me to marry you."

Flattered? After the initial shock, he had been hoping for *happy*, even *excited*, maybe. But as long as she said yes, he would be satisfied. Why was she keeping him in suspense? "Julie, what is your answer?"

"I'm sorry, Erik. But I can't marry you." It was the

last thing she had ever expected to say, if ever she had the good fortune to have him propose to her. Her heart was a ponderous weight in her chest.

He had expected her surprise; he had been ready for her hesitation; he even understood why she had questioned his motives. But nothing had prepared him for an out-and-out refusal. He pulled back to search her face. "You don't want to marry me?"

"I'm sorry. I—can't accept your proposal."

His brows knit in puzzlement. "But you said you loved me!"

"I do love you, Erik," she said gently, sadly. "But that's not enough."

He took hold of that idea. "What would be enough? I'll give you anything that is within my power to give."

She didn't doubt that. He wanted to marry her, and he was a generous man, and a good one. But she was afraid that the one thing she needed from him was beyond his power to give.

His voice softened. "Julie, are you afraid I wouldn't be a good husband? I'll admit I haven't been easy to live with these past weeks, but believe me, that was because of the situation."

"I know. That's not it." He would be a good husband in all the ways that counted, except one.

After a few minutes he said, "I think I know what it is. Your being in love with me isn't enough, because you want me to be in love with you." His voice was flat. "Well, you've got me there. I've made it very clear to you how I feel about love."

He had indeed; and he had also made it clear how he felt about her. If not in words, his actions—protective, caring, tender—betrayed his feelings. If Julie hadn't known it before, she was now all but certain that Erik did indeed love her—but she couldn't *be* certain, unless he admitted it to himself and to her. And he wasn't about to do that.

She stood up. "Yes, I know your feelings, and now you know mine. I'm sorry, Erik, but I can't marry you," she said softly. And then she was gone.

Julie left Isle Anders the next day. She made a plausible excuse to King Ivar and said goodbye to him and Whit at the palace. Because they both knew it would be expected, Erik made the arrangements for her flight and drove her to the airport after breakfast.

He was disinclined to speak and was glad that she said nothing, either. Rejection was never easy, but Julie's refusal had hurt him more deeply than he'd ever imagined.

He pulled up at a remote terminal. "I'll leave you here," he said. He had no intention of treating anyone to any public goodbyes out on the tarmac.

"Of course."

He got her bag out of the back seat and handed it to her. "Thank you for not making a scene at the palace this morning," he said evenly.

"I'll leave it up to you to break the news to your father, when and how you see fit."

"I'm not looking forward to it," he said.

They stood there, face-to-face, a moment too long. Almost against his will he raised his hand and touched her cheek. "I still can't believe you're leaving," he said in a choked voice.

"I have to," she whispered. "Goodbye, Erik." She left then, disappearing through the terminal door.

He got back into the car, swearing. But he didn't drive away. He parked and watched her plane take off and then waited to see if she might have changed her mind. But of the handful of people who walked out of the terminal door, none of them was Julie.

Erik pulled out of the parking lot, swearing again. Did she have to be noble and loyal to the end? Couldn't she have been petty or spiteful, so that he could get some satisfaction out of losing her? Why couldn't she have rejected him by telling him to go to hell, so that he could blow off some steam getting good and mad at her? Better yet, why couldn't she forget about rejecting him at all?

But that would never happen. A woman like Julie would never be able to accept his terms of marriage. He had been right from the beginning—he should have known better than to get mixed up with a woman like her.

Now he was in one hell of a dilemma, thanks to his father's precipitous decision to step down from the throne. Erik was back to square one, and this time the clock was ticking. He had to get married before his coronation. And now that event would not be years distant, as he had always expected.

With a concerted effort, Erik cleared his mind for rational thinking. He was a born problem solver. He would figure out something this time, too.

Without Julie.

The sound of the opening door echoed hollowly throughout the empty castle, making Julie wish she had forgotten her key this time. If she'd had to get Drew to let her in, she would be able to stave off a little longer the loneliness that was waiting to envelope her.

She kicked the heavy door shut behind her and dropped her bag on the floor. Those sounds, too, seemed to reverberate against the far reaches of the stone walls. It had never been like this before. She had lived here alone at the castle for a year and had never been lonely.

But it made sense that nothing would be as it was before. At first she had cursed the timing of the king's announcement, but now she realized it was better that things between her and Erik had been hastened toward their natural conclusion.

Conclusion. It was a dead-end word, and Julie was an open-corridor kind of person. But there were no other avenues to pursue. As much as she loved Erik, when push came to shove she found that she couldn't settle.

It would have been easy to—to marry him and take what he was willing to give her. And what he was willing to give her, at the end, was not inconsiderable. His companionship, humor, strength and intelligence should have been more than enough to sustain her for the rest of her days. He cared for her and would take care of her. He valued her; he enjoyed her; he desired her. He was the only man she ever had or would love, and what was more, she felt that he might love her, too.

But what did it matter what he felt for her, if he kept his feelings locked inside? He wouldn't let himself love her, because allowing himself to love would be to surrender control, to make himself open to losing. The problem wasn't that he didn't love her, but that he didn't *believe.*

And now, now that he had let her go so easily, it looked like he never would.

She picked up her bag and trudged up the stairs to her room in the tower to unpack.

* * *

Erik's work, which was never ending, provided all the excuse he needed to not think about Julie. But he found himself thinking of her at odd times over the next few days, and once he did, his concentration would be interrupted for good.

He looked out the window of his office over the choppy waters of the ocean, toward the west—toward Maine. It would be much better to forget Julie and put his mind to finding a solution to his coronation dilemma. A week had gone by since his father had announced his impending retirement. Erik needed to get married. He needed a woman.

So far he hadn't been able to come up with any possibilities. The only woman that interested him was an impossibility.

Julie went along from day to day, wishing it were September, so she would at least have teaching to occupy her mind. She kept her distance from Drew and Annah, not sure she would ever be ready to talk about what had happened.

There had been no word from Isle Anders, and no reason there should be. Any day she expected to read about Prince Erik's broken engagement in the newspaper. And she braced herself for the inevitable day when the news would hit that he was marrying another woman.

Looking out across the ocean, toward the island that was his home, she realized he had been right. Time and distance had torn the fragile bond they had shared; at least, his end of it. As for her, she knew that time and distance enough did not exist in this world.

* * *

A knock at the door of Erik's office interrupted him as he was engaged in yet another bout of fruitless thought. It was his father. He was looking better each day, Erik noticed. That was a relief, anyway.

The king sat down opposite Erik. "This is for you," he said, putting a package down on the desk.

"What is it?"

"It's a videotape of the night of the ball. I don't believe I ever thanked you for having the cameras there for me."

"It was nothing," Erik said. "Julie made most of the arrangements."

The king settled back in his chair. "How is Julie?" he asked.

Erik decided that, at long last, it was time to come clean with his father. "I don't know," he said, returning the king's steady gaze. "I haven't spoken with her since she returned to Anders Point."

"I see."

"There's something you need to know," Erik told him.

His father waited, silent.

"It's about my engagement to Julie." He stopped, trying to think how best to word it.

At his hesitation, the king said, "I don't know how I could express to you how much your engagement has meant to my recovery."

"Sire," Erik said, "the truth is that Julie and I were never really engaged."

It surprised him that his father showed no surprise. He merely looked thoughtful. When he finally spoke, the king said, "What meant so much was knowing that two people would go to such lengths to do what they thought would help me."

So his father had known all along. And understood

why. "Concern for you was my sole motivation," Erik affirmed.

The king challenged him with those icy blue eyes. "But then things got more complicated," he said.

"Yes," Erik admitted.

"And now Julie is gone. Did you break her heart?"

"I hope not." Erik leaned his elbows on his desk.

"I don't think so. She turned me down when I asked her to marry me, the night of the betrothal feast. But somehow, I still feel like the bad guy."

"You asked her to be your wife? For real?"

"Yes."

"And she refused your proposal?"

"Yes."

"Why?"

Erik didn't want to think about why. He shrugged.

The king pondered that. "I don't have any easy answers for you, my son. She loves you, that much is obvious. And the love of a woman like that is more precious than can be told." He stared out the window.

"I was so blessed, in your mother. We loved each other wholly, completely. Losing her was like being torn in half. You can't imagine the pain I went through." He looked back at Erik. "Or maybe you can."

Erik could. Besides his own grief at the loss of his mother, he had shared the pain of the father he loved. And he was feeling that kind of pain again now. Maybe he hadn't wanted to risk loving Julie because he didn't want to lose her—but he had lost her, anyway.

"My illness has helped me put things in perspective," King Ivar said. "When your mother died, it was as if the sun had been snuffed from my sky. I allowed myself to become immersed in my duties. I knew that she could never be replaced, but I didn't even try to give you and your brother back at least some of the affection you had lost with her passing. In a way I was afraid of getting close to you, because I was afraid of losing you, too. In my pain I forgot what is important.''

Erik found that he was hanging on every word.

His father leaned forward, speaking earnestly. ''As a king, my duty is important. I do want to see the succession secure, but more importantly, I want to have grandchildren. I do want the next queen to be a worthy woman, but more importantly, I want you to be happily married. Your brother, too. Because that is the secret I have found, son,'' he said. ''Compared to the great joy I had during my time with your mother, the pain I suffered at losing her was but a trifle. If I had the chance, I would risk it all again in the blink of an eye. Because I know that there is nothing more important than love.'' And then he left, leaving Erik to his thoughts.

There is nothing more important than love. His mother had surely believed it, and so, he now knew, did his father.

And Julie? He of all people knew how passionately Julie believed in love. Because he had been so fortunate as to win her love, to have her share it with him daily, to feel the power of it.

It had been powerful enough to change his life; to change him. Whether or not he had wanted to, he had finally come to realize that he loved Julie.

He got up from his desk and paced around the office. Why hadn't he seen it before? It explained everything. No wonder he had been sick at heart at losing her. No wonder he had found it impossible to consider looking for another bride. No wonder his life, so enriched by her presence, was so impoverished by her absence.

Now he saw that he had never had a choice in the matter. Loving Julie was his destiny. She had known it from the time she was sixteen, and on some level he had, too. That was why he had run so hard from it.

Love still didn't come with any guarantees. There would always be the risk of losing her someday. But now he knew that far worse was what he was living with now—the pain of having pushed her away, the hollowness of not believing, the stark reality of living day after day without her.

And what he had put her through! She had offered him the most important thing in life—her love—and he had refused it. He no longer cared about the pain he had suffered, considering only the pain he had inflicted. She had given him her heart, and in return he had given her no choice but to turn down his loveless proposal and leave him. After all that, how in the world could he ever hope to have another chance with her?

His gaze fell on the videotape his father had left on the desk. He knew he had to watch it, painful though it would be to relive the events that had occurred that night at the ball: to see Julie; to have the smile that was haunting him in memory there on the screen; to watch her standing with him in the spotlight as he announced their engagement; and then, to see them talking to each other before the kiss. When he got to that part, he rewound the tape and watched it again. The sound hadn't been picked up, of course, but he recalled the conversation. She had agreed to be his fiancée, and he had asked her what, in return, she wanted from him. And she had told him. It was the only thing she had ever asked of him, the word she had whispered right before their lips met in that unforgettable kiss.

Believe.

Erik clicked off the tape, his mind made up. He might not deserve another chance, but he was sure as hell going to take it. And he would just have to believe that it wasn't too late.

Since she had left Isle Anders, Julie had spent more sleepless nights than she cared to think about, but last night was different. She had stayed up to watch the sun rise over the ocean, as usual, but after that she had fallen into a fathoms-deep sleep that lasted well into the morning.

Still groggy, eyes squinting against the bright sunlight streaming through the windows, she stumbled barefoot down the stone staircase and through the bedroom that had been deserted since Erik left. In the bathroom she was brought up short. It couldn't be. She rubbed her eyes and blinked, and still it appeared that someone had used the bathroom after she had the night before. There was a used towel hanging on one of the racks that hadn't been there before.

She was wide awake now, but still she splashed cold water on her face and over most of the T-shirt and shorts she was wearing. The face that looked back at her from the mirror was wide-eyed. No one had been expected. Who was in the castle?

When she stepped back out into the bedroom, she had her answer. Erik's bags stood in one corner, unpacked. He must have arrived that morning, because the bed hadn't been slept in, but beyond a doubt Erik was here.

And he wasn't the only one. A sound out of place drew her to the window. She saw a truck backing up to the kitchen entrance. There were workers out on the lawn, too, and another truck coming up the drive.

She flew downstairs and across the front entrance hall, sidestepping more than one person carrying boxes in the front door. When she pulled up in the doorway to the ballroom, her heart paused in mid-beat.

Standing inside was Erik, pointing and giving directions, looking cool and self-possessed and utterly in charge. Her heart, when it resumed beating, sank. All this could mean only one thing.

Despondent, she turned away, but before she had gone far his voice stopped her.

"Julie!"

He was walking her way, so she summoned up her courage and went forward to meet him in the middle of the ballroom. "Hello, Erik," she said, knowing how hollow her voice must sound and not caring.

"I was wondering when you were finally going to wake up," he said gently, smiling at her.

And she was wondering when he was finally going to tell her that he was marrying someone else. But she had too much pride to say it. She just stuck her chin up and met his gaze, waiting.

To her surprise she saw that his deep brown eyes were soft with tenderness. In a voice that matched them, he said, "Last time we were together, I made you an offer, which you refused." He swallowed.

Time stopped for Julie, while she waited for him to go on.

"I thought it was a pretty good offer," he said. "It was certainly the best I could give you at the time. But now I have a better one." He pulled her into his arms, then lowered his head to kiss her. Right before their lips met, she heard him whisper, "I believe."

Julie, too dazed to return the kiss, broke it off and stared at him. Smiling, he took her shoulders gently and turned her around to look at the ballroom. Amid the general confusion, she began to notice things. A string quartet, taking their instruments out of the cases. Chairs set up for about forty people, no more. The sound of Gustave's voice, booming out orders in the kitchen. A profusion of cheery white and yellow daisies wherever there was room to accommodate them. Off to one side, hanging on a rack, the simple white gown her mother had worn when she had married Julie's father. Out on the side lawn, her mother and father themselves, strolling along and talking with King Ivar.

And standing in front of her, the man she loved, drawing her into his arms again. "What do you think?" he said, his voice reflecting the mixture of hope, fear and daring that runs wild through the heart of a man who has gone out on a limb.

It was her dream wedding. "I didn't even think you were listening," she said, dazed.

"I tried not to," he admitted raggedly. "I tried not to do a lot of things, not to feel things that were a part of me. But I can't do that any longer. I love you, Julie. Please give me a chance to show you how much."

He kissed her on the top of her head. "Because of you, I believe in fairy tales and dreams come true." He kissed her again, on the forehead. "I believe in happily ever after and the pudgy, smiling babies we are going to make together." He kissed her on the nose. "I believe in love at first sight, love that gets stronger when tested and love that lasts for all time, because that is our love."

He kissed her on both cheeks, which were wet now with tears. "I believe. I believe in you. I believe in me. But mostly I believe in you *and* me, now and forever." And then he kissed her on the lips, with reverent tenderness, holding her close to his chest, where she could feel each beat of his pounding heart.

At last he raised his head and looked at her again, searchingly. He didn't say a word, but he was asking her a question.

Her answer was a tremulous smile. "I'll meet you back here at two o'clock," she said.

Epilogue

At two o'clock that day, Julie Britton and Erik Anders took their wedding vows, witnessed by the people in the world who loved them best. Neither one of them made it through without a few tears. Nor did the people who loved them best.

But afterward, at the reception, smiles and laughter reigned. It was a fairy-tale ending, everyone agreed, as they basked in the happiness of the prince and princess. And it was a wonderful beginning, too.

King Ivar stood against one wall, smiling broadly and watching the revelers. His attention was divided between his son and daughter-in-law, who were never far from each other's arms; his other son and Drew Davis, who were positioned on opposite sides of the ballroom; and the exuberant little blond girl who threaded her way among the couples on the dance floor, doing her own private and highly energetic jig.

"What has become of your crown, Your Majesty? I

have never before seen you without it, on such an occasion."

It was Gustave, loyal Gustave, another one of the king's many blessings. He smiled at his old friend. "It seems that I have been charmed out of it by a golden-haired waif."

"Ah. Princess Lexi."

"So she has introduced herself to me, with a very proper curtsy."

"Do not be deceived by her title, Your Majesty. She is the daughter of Drew Davis."

The king was amused by his friend's warning. "I was able to spot the true nature of my son's engagement with Julie," he reminded Gustave. "Leave it to me to discern whether or not Lexi is truly a princess."

Gustave bowed his acquiescence. "I am rather surprised that she found the time speak with you, Your Majesty," he commented. "She has spent half of the afternoon in the kitchen, teasing my staff into feeding her dessert first."

The king smiled. "She has spent the other half coaxing me to join her on the dance floor."

They fell into the comfortable silence of long acquaintance. King Ivar scanned the crowd with the eyes of a master of chess, sensing where all has come from and where it might go, depending upon what strategies came into play. After a while he chuckled to himself.

"You are happy, Your Majesty. It is good to see it."

"Yes, I am happy, Gustave."

"No more worries that there will be no heirs to the throne?"

The king's keen blue eyes swept over to Erik and Julie, who were moving in perfect step, in perfect bliss.

He had not a doubt of their starting a family before long. "No, I am worried no longer," he said.

Then his eyes were drawn back to Whit and his childhood friend Drew, who were studiously avoiding each other. "In fact, Gustave," he added. "I am beginning to think that there was never any reason to worry about the succession."

"Soon you will be playing with your grandchildren."

"Yes. Very soon, I believe," the king answered, chuckling.

And before the song ended, Princess Lexi had succeeded in coaxing His Majesty, King Ivar of Isle Anders, onto the dance floor, with very little trouble indeed.

* * * * *

Don't miss THE PRINCE'S BABY, *the second book in Lisa Kaye Laurel's exciting series,* ROYAL WEDDINGS, *coming this November, only from Silhouette Romance.*

China's greatest love story...

Available for the *first time as a* novel in North America

LOVE IN A CHINESE GARDEN

It's been called China's *Romeo and Juliet.*
Two young lovers are thwarted by an ambitious mother and an arranged marriage. With the help of a clever confidante, they find opportunities to meet...until, inevitably, their secret is revealed.

Can love prevail against danger and separation? Against the scheming of a determined woman?

Find out how to receive a second book absolutely **FREE** with the purchase of **LOVE IN A CHINESE GARDEN!** (details in book)

Available October 1997
at your favorite retail outlet.

Daniel MacGregor is at it again...

New York Times bestselling author

NORA ROBERTS

introduces us to a new generation of MacGregors as the lovable patriarch of the illustrious MacGregor clan plays matchmaker again, this time to his three gorgeous granddaughters in

From Silhouette Books

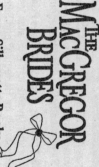

THE MACGREGOR BRIDES

Don't miss this brand-new continuation of Nora Roberts's enormously popular *MacGregor* miniseries.

Available November 1997 at your favorite retail outlet.

NRMB-S

DIANA WHITNEY

Continues the twelve-book series 36 HOURS in September 1997 with Book Three

OOH BABY, BABY

In the back of a cab, in the midst of a disastrous storm, Travis Stockwell delivered Peggy Saxon's two precious babies and, for a moment, they felt like a family. But Travis was a wandering cowboy, and a fine woman like Peggy was better off without him. Still, she and her adorable twins had tugged on his heartstrings, until now he wasn't so sure that *he* was better off without *her.*

For Travis and Peggy and *all* the residents of Grand Springs, Colorado, the storm-induced blackout was just the beginning of 36 Hours that changed *everything!* You won't want to miss a single book.

Silhouette®

Look us up on-line at: http://www.romance.net

36HRS3

**Beginning in September
from Silhouette Romance...**

THE BRUBAKER BRIDES

a new miniseries by
Carolyn Zane

They're a passel of long, tall, swaggering cowboys who
need tamin'...and the love of a good woman. So y'all
come visit the brood over at the Brubaker ranch and
discover how these rough and rugged brothers got
themselves hog-tied and hitched to the marriage wagon.

The fun begins with
MISS PRIM'S UNTAMABLE COWBOY (9/97)

"No little Miss Prim is gonna tame me! I'm not about to
settle down!"
   —Bru "nobody calls me Conway" Brubaker
"Wanna bet?"
   —Penelope Wainwright, a.k.a. Miss Prim

The romance continues in
HIS BROTHER'S INTENDED BRIDE (12/97)

"Never met a woman I couldn't have...then I met my
brother's bride-to-be!"
   —Buck Brubaker, bachelor with a problem
"Wait till he finds out the wedding was never really on...."
   —the not-quite-so-engaged Holly Fergusson

And look for Mac's story coming in early '98 as
THE BRUBAKER BRIDES series continues, only from

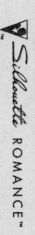

Silhouette ROMANCE™